WICKLOW
FOLK
TALES

WICKLOW
FOLK
TALES

BRENDAN NOLAN

The History Press Ireland

For Dolores

First published 2013

The History Press Ireland
50 City Quay
Dublin 2
Ireland
www.thehistorypress.ie

British Library Cataloguing in Publication Data.
A catalogue record for this book is available from the British Library.

ISBN 978 1 84588 785 8

Typesetting and origination by The History Press

CONTENTS

ACKNOWLEDGEMENTS

Sean Ó Cinneide and Cáit, Margaret Byrne, Mick Whelan, John and Molly Keogh and family, Pidge Byrne, Pat Fleming, Danielle Allison, Liz Weir, Nuala Hayes, Niall Reddy, Aideen McBride, John Gaffney and John Keane, for their help, and encouragement; not forgetting Rita, Rachel, Josh, Holly, Leo and Luci.

INTRODUCTION

In Wicklow you may come across a storyteller on a quiet road, at a crossroads, in a library, at a storytelling event, or in many other places, and when you least expect it. Long ago, when people did their week's shopping after church on Sundays to avoid another long journey into town, stories tumbled out of the back of the church after Mass and along village streets, in and out of tiny shops crammed with neighbours all buying in for the week ahead and looking for something to reflect on in the quiet countryside of the everyday.

You may not at first recognise a storyteller if you meet one, for they can be of any age, gender, or disposition. They will listen to you for a while, with respect for your own told tales, before gently launching into a narrative drawn from their own seasoned store of traditional stories. Many will lightly tell a tale of a recent happening to someone you may well recognise, though slightly disguised to allow for a little creativity in the telling. Or, they may recall a story that has come through the oral tradition of the county.

During the story, you may smile at authority that has been got the better of; sigh at a wrong done to someone else; delight in evil outdone or in the escape of the virtuous. You may wonder whether, if you were to seek for gold in the Gold Mines river, you would become rich, or would you find that the treasure turns to leaves in your hand, a trick of the Good People? Would the sudden appearance of a demonic figure above cause you to throw your heels in the air as you fled? Or, would you return when all was quieted, once more?

Even a doubting listener will pay attention to the teller when he recounts a tale of valour or duplicity that happened perhaps in the year of insurrection, or in the hunted years following failed rebellion, or perhaps in a winter snowstorm, or on a drowsy summer's day in the high hills, in the century just past.

The May Day tradition may be recalled of a bush dressed up with gathered egg shells, with wild yellow flowers and ribbons placed upon it. Candles or rush lights would light up the bush and, when the lights burnt out, the bush itself, usually a dry gorse bush pulled from the soil of the mountain, would be set alight.

May Day was a significant time in community life. Many contracts for work and land began on this day. For some, the sight of a May bush brought a feeling of protection against unseen forces that might visit from an earlier time and different beliefs.

One tradition holds that snow lying on Croghan Kinsella (the gold mountain) on May Day is so bad an omen that local farmers would expect their landlord to forego the rent for the coming half-year.

Whatever story is told it will be energised by the teller until both listener and teller are almost transformed into the subject and time, without knowing how or why. Perhaps, the listener will see an ephemeral light floating towards them on a dark road in a glen where no person has lived in a few hundred years, and will wait to hear their fate.

Of course, neither they nor the person in the story will consider putting a world of space and time between them and the oncoming brightness; for to do so will mean they will not hear the story.

What happens?

Even if the story has been heard before, the listener's memory slips. A skilled tradition-bearer will make the story sound as if it is the first time it has been told, and only to the present ears of the gathered-in listeners.

For it will be the only time that the story is told in this form. The oral tradition is such that while the essence of the story remains true, the nuances of the story will sough and sigh according to time and circumstance. A brief moment of telling will include only the essence of the story, longer time will allow for more profuse elucidation.

And while Irish culture abounds with new storytellers, and stories are being recalled in many places, there is an onus on the present generation to gather stories from older tellers to carry along the tradition of storytelling. For, no matter how wise a storyteller may be, all are humanly fallible and voices will be stilled in time.

Two of the stories in this collection came from Mick Whelan, a melodious storyteller who lived deep in the glens of Wicklow.

Mick would say that two stories are twice as good as one, and one better than none at all, for he was a joyful storyteller; but his was an oral collection committed to memory and his store of stories lies with him. *Ar dheis Dé* go *raibh a anam dílis.*

Storytelling is from memory; for storytellers do not read out stories, which is a different pastime and skill. But stories need to be collected and the history of a people kept safe for those yet to be born. And to echo the voices of those now silent. It is said that every great storyteller is also a great listener. It behoves those of us now alive to listen and to gather stories as a people's treasure.

If any of the stories in this collection move you to tell them to someone else, then do so, for you will have joined a long line of storytellers through the millennia, for story is all.

Tell true, tell well, and enjoy the story.

Brendan Nolan
www.irishfolktales.com

1

AN ARMY
OF STONES

When a mist rolls across a Wicklow hill and clings to every rock and wind-battered tree on the bare hillside, and all is silent for miles around, it is all too easy to believe that a shape looming out of the fog is not an inanimate object but a fellow human being.

There is a foothill on the way up to the brooding mass of Lugnaquilla Mountain at the head of the Ow Valley that is called Farbreaga, from the Irish expression *fear bréige*, meaning a false man, in the sense of not being real. The term is commonly applied to a rock or heap of stones resembling a man, though some call scarecrows that they make with their own hands by the same name.

Michael Dwyer, one of the leaders of the resistance following the failed 1798 insurrection, sought refuge in the almost impenetrable natural fortress of wild hill and woodland that was the Wicklow of his day. John Sheil of Carrignamuck, many years later, recalled a local story of that time, when Dwyer was being hunted by Yeomen, civilian volunteers who used government arms and uniforms to police their seditious neighbours. Dozens of loyalist Yeomanry corps had been raised in Wicklow to put down nationalist unrest.

Dwyer was headed over Farbreaga on the way to his redoubt in his native Glen of Imaal on the far side of Lugnaquilla, with Yeomen in pursuit. When he was part of the way up the foothill he

put hats on the rocks that were scattered across it. He then commenced firing down the slope and, by moving about, fooled the pursuers into thinking he had a number of associates with him on the hillside. The Yeomen fled.

His is not the only story of mistaken identification to do with Farbreaga.

Julia Doyle of nearby Ballygobbin recalled for the Schools Folklore Commission, in 1938, that one dark moonless night, a man coming alone from Farbreaga through the soft slippery bog saw a light coming towards him. Thinking it might be someone he knew, he halted in readiness to greet the bearer of the light, which he took to be a lantern in the hand. But, to his unsettled surprise, the light went out when it reached him and lit up once more once it had passed. He stared and stared but could see no human form to the side of the moving light. There was no one to whom he could ascribe a neighbourly trick being playing on him.

Such are the tricks of light that can betray the mind on a dark Wicklow hillside. And who is to say who is moving about there?

September is, on average, the month with most sunshine on Farbreaga. Rainfall has no distinct peak month, which means that in any part of the year it is never far from rain and a great many swirling mists. People may see things that might or might not be there.

In 1913 two men were out ferreting rabbits on the mountain. They shouldn't have been doing so for they were on private land. The ferret most used in Ireland then was descended from the European polecat; the ferret was encouraged into the rabbit hole from where it chased the rabbit out and into a trap or net spread by the human trapper who then killed it and the rabbit was taken either for personal use or sold to a local butcher.

There was not much of a mist that night but it was dark from the clouds scudding across the moonlit sky. One of the men straightened up from setting a trap and started in surprise, for through the gloom there on a rock higher up the slope of the hill, he saw a man standing looking down at them. There might have been nothing unusual, except that he recognised the man and knew that he had been dead for twenty years. He remembered being at his wake as a lad, gadding about the kitchen trying to steal pipes of tobacco.

The man was dressed just as he had been on the night when he was laid out on the way to the grave. He wore corduroy trousers and a white flannel jacket, and his whiskers were shaved off. A youngish man then, he was father to the man who now owned the mountain and kept sheep on it. There was no doubt in both the poachers' minds as to the man they saw standing on the slope above them. But, truth to tell, they were poachers, and, technically speaking, if they took the matter further it would be they themselves who ended up in the Petty Sessions in Rathdrum. The poachers had no desire to see the inside of the courthouse in the matter of rabbits and the appearance of a *fear bréige*.

Just as they had no desire to argue with any living man on the rights or wrongs of what they were about, so neither of them had any interest in discussing the issue with a ghost from the other world.

They ran as fast as their slithering feet would carry them, across the sheep tracks of the hill, leaving the rabbit traps and ferret to their own devices. They ran and ran, not reaching their homes until day was beginning to break.

One of the men took to his bed for three days and would not stir, no matter what was said to him, or what cajoling was put to him or what was offered to him.

His accomplice was made of sterner stuff in daylight and felt emboldened to return the next day to retrieve the ferret and the tools of their nocturnal trade. He did so, and returned home with no further incident to report. For safety sake, they moved onto other ground in their hunt for rabbits, for it was an onerous enough task without having to engage with ghosts on the hill.

Others also had experiences in the hunt for rabbits on Farbreaga. However, while there is no preternatural report of how the following incident came about, it is chastening to think of the strength of character that compelled local man James Whelan to drag his injured self across the hill in the winter of 1930.

The 58-year-old family man was out rabbit hunting in the area and found his way up onto Farbreaga, an area with which he was very familiar. He knew where the rabbit burrows were located that were to be seen by the casual hunter; but he also knew where other entrances were hidden by rocks and folds of the land.

He prised up rocks to let his ferret get down to the rabbits and all went well for a time. But rocks on the mountain sometimes seem to be governed by a different agency. One rounded rock that he moved seemed to have settled safely in its new place and so he took his hands away from it to catch hold of the ferret, and to let it slip down into the revealed hole. But no sooner had he turned away than the rock slid down the incline towards him, according to his son Mick Whelan who related the story, many years later.

The rock shifted and in the ensuing tumbling of stone and body the rock broke the man's hip and rolled on to settle in a new hollow. It was a simple accident, perhaps, but life-threatening in consequence; for James was on his own, except for his ferret and

his sheepdog who was never far from his heels on his walks across
the hills of his native county.

He lay there in agony as darkness surrounded him on the hill
and the temperature dropped, as rapidly as a stone tumbling down
the cliff face on Lugnaquilla in the distance. It grew colder as darkness spread and a frost formed, the darkness bringing a shivering
cold to the helpless man.

Painfully he took off his tie and draped it around the dog's neck
and tried to send it home so that his family would recognise the
tie and come searching for him. But the dog refused to leave him;
it chose to stay with its master rather than go home without him.

While this was going on, the ferret emerged from the rabbit's
hole. James reached over to the squirming animal. He caught it

and placed it back into his bag in a moment of calm not unknown at times of great peril.

James lay and considered his options: it was a choice of lying there on the hill and freezing to death from shock and low temperature, or trying to get himself across to a farmhouse he had passed on the way up the valley.

Steeling himself against the excruciating pain, he began to drag himself across the ridge of the hill on his way to assistance. His legs were not only useless to him, but the banging against scree and rock sent shafts of pain running through his tormented body.

His hands and upper body were all that could help him on his never-ending journey across the hard frozen ground. His progress was slow as he measured his path inch by inch, with long breaks in between as the pain threatened to overcome him and knock him unconscious.

Daylight came slowly and he was still on the hill, keeping to the high ground so he could drift downwards when he came to the house; for he feared that climbing upwards dragging a broken-hipped body would be beyond his strength and ability. If he lost height he would not be able to rise up again and would most likely perish among the boulders strewn about the undulating surface of the hill.

All day long he kept going as best he could. If his family and neighbours were out looking for him they were searching in the wrong places, not surprisingly, since he had wandered about somewhat in his quest for rabbits on the previous day.

Night came on once more as he made his way down to the yard of the farmhouse. By then he was unable to call out, or, even to make it as far as the door of the house.

He came to a halt in the farmyard as a fatal coldness spread through his body. To have come so far and to feel his life ebbing away must have been hard to contemplate for this man of the mountains.

However, just as all hope seemed lost, fortune turned in his favour for the farmer came out with a lantern to check his animals before the family retired for the night. He did his rounds and was on his way back inside the house when he saw or heard, or sensed, something unusual in the darkness. His light held aloft showed him the battered and exhausted body of James lying in a dark heap on the ground.

He was immediately brought into the house, where the welcoming warmth of the homestead began his recovery. They tended him there overnight, having first sent word to his anxious family that he had been found alive after two nights on the hillside of Farbreaga.

When daylight came, they placed him on a cart and brought him down the rugged track to the public road and his home. Many years later, when his ordeal and courage had rolled itself into local folklore, a recovered James said that the bumping and swaying of the cart on the rutted track caused more pain than had the dragging odyssey across the hill.

2

A HAND IN
THE NIGHT

Some humans show a remarkable bravado when dealing with matters beyond their ken, like digging for gold in a fairy rath or playing tricks on others in a graveyard at a time of internment, or encountering the Devil while searching for a missing daughter.

There is a rath on Ballygobbin hill in the south of Wicklow county where a number of men, a few years ago, decided it would be a fine idea to dig down and to take for themselves some of the gold that was reputed to be there.

The men dug down into the ground and soon had a decent sized depression hollowed out, but not a sight of anything remotely resembling gold to be found. Disheartened, the gold seekers decided to take a short rest on the surrounding soft grass. One of the men, however, would not give up so easily and continued with his labour.

Imagine his surprise when, looking up from his digging, he saw a dark figure on the bank, staring down at him without a stir or a word out of him.

In many folktales a devil or some such other-worldly manifestation is often depicted as a frightful image of a being who is black from head to foot, and with red eyes. Thus it was that the man in the hole was naturally fearful and immediately leapt out of the declivity and took off running, all the way home, a race he won from his equally terrified companions who followed him down the hill, in some haste.

Word soon spread as to what had happened. Others who were a little less fearful, not having seen the apparition in the first place, wandered up to the site to see if any gold had been disturbed in the men's flight and if it might be lying around the place.

They did not stir in that direction until the next morning, however, until light had touched all parts of the glen and few shadows remained. For if they were avaricious they were not foolish with it. However, when the first people arrived at the spot, they found the hole already filled in, by whom not one person alive could or would say, ever afterwards.

It had been the image of the strange and unexpected that had caused the rout of the gold diggers; that, and the certainty somewhere in their collective folk memories of strange beings lurking at the edge of darkness.

The rath was left undisturbed for a long time after that and may be undisturbed yet, for who knows who stands guard over such things, in the remote parts of the county.

There was a farmer in a different place in Wicklow who had a high-spirited and beautiful daughter who needed careful guarding. She needed to be kept away from the amorous advances of the local bucks who, given half a chance, were bent on mischief with the enthralled teenager.

Electricity was not long come to that part of the country as part of the rural electrification scheme that saw most houses hooked up to the national grid, for better or for worse. The farmer had installed electric lighting in the barn as well as in the family dwelling, for he was a far-seeing man. The switch was placed on the wall next to the old tin door. The door was troublesome in that it had never quite fitted the space given over to it, but it meant that a hand could come through a gap and switch the light on or off from the outside, depending on whether a person was coming or going.

On this particular night, the daughter and her latest boyfriend were sporting themselves inside the building, out of the winter darkness and snowy wind. The farmer heard a noise as he was passing through the yard and turned to investigate. He called out advance warning to any tramp or thief who might be inside the barn.

His daughter was surprised to hear her father's voice calling out in the darkness and her beau, not wishing to be caught in such a compromising situation and face the wrath of an angry father, looked around wildly for means of escape, but there was none. He could but wait for discovery and reckoning, not to mention banishment from the girl's company. Quite unexpectedly, however, providence took a hand.

The farmer, apprehensive of who or what might be lurking inside his barn, sneaked his hesitant hand into the gap beside the ill-fitting door to reach for the electricity switch. At that moment, in a spontaneous attempt to delay the inevitable, the young man reached out and grabbed the farmer's wrist.

The man outside the barn only knew that a grip had closed around his wrist in the darkness. He howled out in fear, for who knew if a red-eyed being was inside trying to draw him in, for who knew what? The young man inside held his breath so as not to cry out in fear himself, for he was in the dark as to what was happening, albeit on the inside of the old draughty building with a willing companion who was by now hanging onto him in her own paroxysm of fear (and something else). The man that was her father was outside howling in dread and the younger man inside was struggling with a hand that had appeared through the gap.

Freeing himself suddenly, her father ran for the house and his legally held shotgun to discharge a shot into the air to see if that might redress the balance of terror. If what was inside the barn was human it would be scared by the loud report of the gun going off. If not, then the farmer's neighbours would be alerted to the state of affairs and might be expected to come to his call for assistance.

The couple in the barn heard the farmer running away and the girl realised all too quickly that her father had left only to return with some other stratagem to deal with the being in his barn.

She told the boy to open the door, leaving the light off for safety, and to make his getaway home across the fields and out of harm's way, for a shotgun, while deadly at close quarters, would do little enough harm to a fleeing lover a few fields away from the scene.

In the meantime, she stood well back from the farmhouse door as her father emerged in the spilling light with a loaded gun and a new determination to face his tormentor. He passed by his daughter in the shadows, without seeing her. And when he was well away, she stepped backwards into the light and shouted at him to be careful.

The farmer, surprised to see her stepping out of the house behind him, for he had not seen her in there when he had fetched his gun, told her to stay in the house where she would be safe.

With an audience to play to, the farmer made a show of calling out to the tormentor in the barn, but got no response, of course, as the disappointed buck was away by then.

The farmer reached gingerly inside the barn, pressed the light switch and bathed the scene in a weak yellow light. He spent a good deal of time inside the building while his frustrated daughter shivered on the step, as the perspiration from her earlier excitement dried on her body and her evening's fun departed with the disappearing heels of the lad of her dreams.

Her father refrained from firing the gun in the barn, as it was clear to him that whatever had been in there had now departed. Like many a father before, or since, he stopped to study his daughter on the way back in, for there was something about her demeanour that did not quite sit right. Somewhere in his mind was a suspicion as to how she had appeared behind him when she had not been before him on his hurried arrival into the house for his shotgun.

Not for the first time, he was sorry that her mother had passed away many years before, for if there is one thing that a father finds hard to fathom it is a wilful daughter.

The night passed peacefully enough; even if it was disturbed by the daughter's tossing and turning for a long time in her single and solitary bed.

The next day, the farmer told his neighbours what had happened. Most agreed that it was unlikely it was a red-eyed devil or goblin that had been about the place in the dark. But, equally, there had been no sightings of any strangers in the locality for some time.

That was enough for the farmer, for if there is one place where a stranger moving through the countryside will be seen it is in the mountains where the footfall of a visitor is noticed by many, and known to all, soon enough.

Suspicion soon fell on the daughter and her last known boyfriend; but, when both were questioned, they so strongly denied all knowledge of the other's existence that it only served to confirm the farmer's suspicion that he had been the victim of a hoax. Intentional or not, it mattered little in its result, for it was not long before his peers started to pull his leg about being caught by the wrist by a devil in his own yard.

There was even talk for a while about recollections of a man called Peter Doyle of Redcross, who had appeared at the Avoca & Rathdrum Sessions in January 1875 on a similar matter: Doyle was charged with annoying a James Cullen and his family by rapping at Cullen's house and by his actions putting everyone in the household in fear of their lives. However, no one could trace a line of descent from him to the young man currently under suspicion.

In any case, after a while, the young man's fancy wandered away to a less troublesome household and a young softy of a woman therein. The farmer's daughter aged by the day and was not as amenable as she had once been to hiding in a draughty barn with a lad who her father was intent on sending to meet the dark figure with the red fiery eyes.

The silent watcher standing by the ditch might or might not have been observing the proceedings in the farmyard on that black night, when something reached out of the darkness and grabbed an unsuspecting man by the wrist, just a few steps from his own home.

Such are the sights to be seen on a dark Wicklow night when strange tales are about.

3

THE RESURRECTION
OF SEAN

Wicklow abounds in stories of confusion, mistake and mischief.

Sean did not own his land, but paid another person rent for the privilege of living and working on the property. At the time of this story, Sean was unable to pay the rent. Non-payment made forfeiture of his holding inevitable and so the landlord gave Sean a week's notice to leave.

Sean had two stacks of corn in hand when he was told to leave. The corn could generate some ready revenue for him, so he, along with two kindly neighbours, threshed it and Sean then took his leave to travel to market with the oats, hoping to sell to the highest bidder and return with funds for the family.

He was well on his way when he met a man who asked what Sean had with him in the cart. Sean showed the oats to the man, who tested them and offered to buy them for almost nothing. Sean refused with a great show of disinterest in the offer. The man increased his offer a little. Sean came down a small bit in his asking price. It went on that way until they finally agreed on a bargain of £5 for the lot.

It is after this exchange that the story takes a strange turn. For whether Sean lost his way home, or decided to 'take a drop for the road', it seems he did not immediately return home with his newly found funds.

That is, according to Luke Ford, of Knocanoocra, who was 60 years of age when he related the story for the Schools Folklore

Collection taken up in the 1930s by primary school pupils who collected stories from older people in the community.

As the story goes, for some strange reason Sean's wife, after some days, declared Sean dead and proceeded to have a wake for him in their house, around a closed coffin.

Neighbours came to pay their respects; the landlord was informed of Sean's passing and was asked to stay the termination of the family's lease, which he did for a while, being a man of standing in the Church.

The coffin was buried in the parish graveyard, with full solemnity, by the local priest, who said Sean had been a fine family man whose every thought was for his family's care, and who should be remembered in the prayers of all present for the repose of his sweet soul. Everyone nodded their head and agreed to do so, at least for the moment. And that was that.

It was not long after Sean's burial that he arrived home, a little the worse for wear but otherwise hale and hearty and, most importantly, alive.

It was a dark night when he walked into the yard. The house was dim and quiet when he lifted the latch and stepped into the little home, with just a glow from the hearth where some neighbours had brought sods of turf to see the bereaved through their time of torment.

Sean made his way to where the small family lay asleep, their arms wrapped around one another for comfort and warmth. A considerate man, rather than disturb the slumbering bodies he went to sleep out in the barn, intending to return the following morning, Sunday, to join the others for a stirabout breakfast before walking to Mass in the church, a few miles away.

He found a comfortable spot for himself in the barn and dozed off, content that he was home and that the few shillings left in his purse would satisfy the rent. Waking early the next morning, with the light spilling around him, Sean heard someone moving about the yard and sat up to see who was about at such an early hour. He peered out of the door to see a pair of bailiffs attempting to take his last remaining pig away in settlement of rent arrears.

He knew both of the bailiffs well, and they him, from the many conversations they'd had over slow payment of rent on the holding.

Annoyed by their avaricious manner, Sean grabbed a nearby pitchfork and erupted from the barn in a fury to chase the two men away.

Both of them had been at his funeral several days earlier and did not linger to argue over rent arrears with an aroused ghost, who was advancing on them with what looked like a trident borrowed from the Devil.

They did not look back until they were the best part of an Irish mile away, and glad to be alive and able to relate that the ghost of Sean had returned to haunt the little farm on the hill. What the landlord was going to make of the story was another matter.

His success at seeing off the bailiffs so easily puzzled Sean, as the two men had a tough reputation and he had expected a shouting match, at the very least.

That the bailiffs had run away from him would be a nice little boast to make to his wife. But when he entered the house, it was empty. This was a situation that perplexed Sean, who had hoped for a welcome home, at least. However, he noticed that the children's boots were missing, so he realised they were away to Sunday Mass, as it was the only time in the week when they were not allowed to go barefoot. When they returned from church, the boots would be put away for another week.

So, Sean stepped out in the direction of the church and hoped that the first reading of the gospel would not be over by the time he got there; he would technically have missed Mass on that account even if he stayed for the rest. That was the rule and, if broken, absolution had to be sought in confession, as soon as possible, or risk dying beforehand with an unclean soul. Such was the way people lived their lives in Ireland of a hundred years ago.

It was later than he thought by the time Sean made off down the lane. He skipped along the empty road, for on Sunday mornings everyone moved in the same direction towards the church, returning later on from the other direction. There is a point in between these two migrations where the road is empty and nothing stirs.

It was along this deserted road that Sean made his determined way. It would be a good opportunity to meet his two neighbours who had helped thresh the corn and thank them for their assistance. He would be glad to reassure his wife also that they were once more in funds.

There was a tradition at Irish Sunday Masses that children and women sat on one side of the church, while menfolk and older boys sat on the other. Outside, in the porch, spilling out into the open air were more men who were present in body only, but who occupied their minds with other things until Mass was concluded.

Some claimed they were following a tradition that an outer ring of men kept watch for priest hunters, as during the Penal Days when it was an offence to celebrate Mass. They stood guard and would raise the alarm, delaying the pursuers until the priest got away.

However, when Sean happened down the road it had been many a year since anyone had kept watch for a foreigner at an Irish Mass. He turned into the churchyard with a greeting for some old school companions, quite unaware that he had been buried out of this same church not a week since, and so was surprised when the worshippers fell away from him in silent dread. Some took to their bicycles and abandoned all semblance of worship as they made their speedy way home. They could shrive their souls at confession on the following Saturday.

Very soon, the remaining faithful had also left the church, including Sean's little family who were swept out in the confusion when the priest announced that Mass was suspended for the moment, while he faced a challenge of faith, there inside the church. Pretty soon there was only the priest and a pair of terrified altar boys, in black surplices and white soutanes, facing the bewildered Sean.

With what authority the priest could muster, he asked Sean what he wanted of him, this day. Sean said he'd come for Mass and to see his family and was sorry he was late but thought, as he eyed the witnessing altar boys, that his lateness might wait until Saturday next in the confessional.

The priest had not undergone seven years of intensive training to be bested by a dead man apologising for missing the first reading of the gospel. He dismissed the altar boys, who exited with alacrity.

Sean answered the priest's questions as to where he had travelled with the oats and where he had been afterwards, some details of which escaped Sean entirely in recall, in fairness. He was more than a little surprised when the priest told him he had been buried in the graveyard on his wife's say-so. She had asked that his coffin not be opened. The priest added that his wife would be shocked to see him, no less than the fleeing congregation.

Sean was somewhat nonplussed and apologised but said he would return on the morrow, Monday, to dig himself back up and make restitution to the graveyard; but, for now he was anxious to call on the landlord to pay the arrears on the family's holding.

The priest agreed to this but did not bother to send word to the landlord of Sean's mission, for the landlord was of a different persuasion and it was none of the priest's business to call on him at home.

The unfortunate landlord had already been primed by his terrorised bailiffs about the arrival of a demon. So, when Sean walked into the pebbled yard, the landlord gave instructions that he be allowed in by the front door and not by the back scullery door, where tenants generally knocked when there on business.

By now Sean had become used to the reaction of the living to his reappearance and said nothing at all to the landlord when he was asked in a trembling voice what his business might be there.

Instead, Sean held out a cloth-wrapped package with the money therein. The gesture had a surprising effect on the man who claimed Sean's land as his own. He fell to his knees and swore he would not take the money from the widow and her poor family. What's more, they could all stay on the small farm rent free for the rest of their lives, and would that satisfy Sean and would he go away and not return again?

Sean nodded assent and walked out in silence. All that could be heard was the crunching of his departing feet on the landlord's driveway.

He decided not to return to his own home that night, not until he saw the contents of the coffin. Next morning, as soon as the eight o'clock Massgoers had departed and all was quiet, he began to dig. The freshly disturbed soil was easily removed and he soon had the box hoisted out of the grave. Inside, he found a large lump of bog oak that had accounted to the pall bearers for the weight on their shoulders in the funeral procession.

He removed it and donated the empty coffin to the priest for the use of any mendicant parishioner who turned up dead. The bog oak he left for another day's work while he set his gaze towards the hill and his little rent-free farm – and his impatient wife who had given up his ghost before he was ready to do so himself.

There was a conversation to be had between them, at the every least. On the way home he stopped at the crossroads shop and bought sugarsticks for the children from a quaking shopkeeper. The children would be glad to see him (and the sugarsticks), that much he knew.

As for the rest, he would have to wait and see.

4

THE TRAVELS
OF DAVY

The following tale, of a Wicklow farmer's son who caused great misunderstanding when he asked another man for work, is recounted according to a story told a good many years ago by John Wheatly, a 50-year-old farmer from Slieverue, to his grandson.

Davy was an unruly boy, both in the house and at work around the family farm. If there was an argument, or someone to be the cause of an argument, Davy was sure to be in the middle of it.

It came to a head, one day when his father arrived in from the fields and Davy, as usual, was driving everyone mad with his she-nanigans. His father took him to one side and spoke to him, not entirely harshly, for he remembered his own days as a youngster on the local hills and glens when no dare was refused, no danger too great to chance, and no pot left unstirred if some amusement could be had from it. But he made it clear that Davy had reached the day when it was his turn to leave home and to seek his fortune elsewhere. Perhaps, in the future, when all was settled at home and Davy had some wider experience of the world, he could return and they could all live happily together.

In readiness, his father had set aside some savings that Davy was welcome to take with him on his journey, or at least a por-tion of the fortune, his father added, lest anyone be listening and be moved to raise a ruction about the fatted calf being sent off with Davy.

To be honest, Davy was delighted to be away from the place, for he had long since decided that once his hat was on, his roof was thatched and it was time to seek his fortune elsewhere. He knew there were many places where he could easily settle down in his own right. But, before that he would engage in as many adventures as he could manage to find.

Nonetheless, he played the part of the dutiful son and asked his father if he thought he was ready to go on the road on his own account. His father assured him he was and said it would be best to leave in a couple of days, to allow everyone to become used to the fact that he was going away.

Davy agreed, and for the next day or so was polite to everyone. In return, everyone was polite to him, for no one wanted to part company on bad terms; though truth to tell, everyone, including Davy and his father, was counting the hours until he was gone from among them.

His father took the time to tell him a few manly truths that Davy already knew, but he paid the older man the honour of believing that he had never thought of such things in such a way before.

Then came the day. Davy rose early, made some tea and ate a thick cut of currant bread with fresh butter slathered across it. He put some tea in a tommy can and stuck a corner of bread in his other pocket. Pressing the latch gently, he stepped through the familiar yard and down the rutted drive to the road, and away he went.

He found he was not in much of a hurry to find work. Like many another before him, Davy enjoyed himself along the way and found a great many companions who were happy to spend his fortune with him in the drinking houses along the road.

Nevertheless, the day soon came when he had an empty pocket, and Davy realised he was hungry enough to eat a feed and a half. However, he didn't have any coins left in his purse. And he found that his credit had ended in all the places where he had been welcome, just a short while before. There was nothing for it but to take up a living once more.

By now, his peregrinations had brought him into Dublin county, which at that time was surrounded by a rural hinterland with plenty of Dubliners following the farming trade of their fathers before them. Davy thought he might find among them enough work for one man.

He arrived at an establishment that combined a farmhouse with a big house. He was told that the farm had a manager who was seeking a worker with exactly the skills Davy had to offer. It seemed that all he had to do was ask for the job and it would be his.

He arrived at the manager's office door just as the man was leaving on business. Davy made himself known and said he understood there was a position to be filled and wondered if he might be considered for the job. He went on to list his experience, while the manager walked away from him towards a horse and trap that would take him on his way to a fair.

The older man paused to study Davy before he boarded the trap and said he would speak to him when he returned. And then the farm manager was off in the trap, clip-clopping down the road on his master's business, leaving Davy wondering what he should do next.

Davy wandered about the farmyard for a while, but since it was a working day, everyone was out and about in the fields or elsewhere at their tasks. He spoke to one man who answered questions in so many monosyllables that Davy gave up and strolled away. He found himself in the nearest field, where he saw a figure leaving by the kitchen of the big house, across the field from the farmyard wherein lay the manager's office.

It was the figure of a butler, dressed in a worn uniform and with the gait of a man intent on his own business. He was headed straight towards Davy.

Instinctively, Davy hid before the butler had a chance to catch sight of him. When the man changed direction and went around to the back of the manager's office, Davy followed quietly after him.

Behind the buildings was a stone cupboard, or press, with an old cracked wooden door that had been green at one time but was now more of a camouflage shade, with blotches missing where summer suns had blistered and popped the old paint. The door was overhung with green trailing ivy, its dusty leaves hiding the door from most passers-by.

To his amusement, Davy saw the butler put a bottle of whiskey and a roasted goose into the press before carefully pushing the door back into its socket and rearranging the foliage around it. Before he closed it entirely he took something else from the press, a purse perhaps, and hid it beneath a bundle of straw lying on the ground nearby.

The butler was about to leave when the unmistakable sound came of the trotting pony returning. Davy saw the butler conceal himself beneath some loose hay, rather than strike back across the open space to the big house. He wondered why the man had hidden the food and drink. And what had he taken from the press to hide? That the man was up to no good was clear; but since Davy had not met him before he was reluctant to settle on a final opinion about the surreptitious man.

Davy stepped into the yard and unyoked the pony while the manager quizzed him about his origins, his breeding and generation and his capabilities if he were to be retained as a farm worker on the estate. Davy answered as truthfully as he could, and where there was conflict between the truth and reality he fashioned a lie that was acceptable to his interrogator. In the heel of the hunt, the farm manager and Davy struck a bargain and Davy was hired. He was hungry from the lack of food over the preceding few days and so asked the manager if he could have something to eat to keep his strength up until the evening meal was laid out.

However, the farm manager said he was a busy man and that he did not provide food for the workers himself. In any case, he said, there was none to be had until later on, when it would be sent down from the house.

But Davy, ever mischievous, said he knew where there was a fine goose to be had. The manager looked at him askance before asking where this might be, for he was already wondering if he had done the right thing by hiring a stranger.

Davy brought him around to where the press lay hidden, opened the door a little and produced the cooked goose to the astonishment of the farm manager.

To wash it down he pulled out the brimming bottle of whiskey, at which the manager began to wonder who Davy really was, to be able to so easily produce food and drink at the drop of a hat in the middle of a working day. He grew very uneasy and stepped away from Davy, the better to study him.

Davy offered the manager the first swig from the bottle. He took it to see what it was like. As soon as the spirits rose to the top of his skull, the farm manager knew that he would not keep Davy on in the job. For who could trust a man with such strong drink in his pocket?

Davy realised the job was lost, for it did not do to better your employer with superior knowledge on the first day. In which case, he continued to tear lumps off the goose and devour it, while pouring as much whiskey in after it as his system would absorb in the time available.

If the farm manager was frightened by now, Davy reserved his final flourish for the poor man when he picked up a pitchfork and asked if he would like to see him rise the Devil?

Unable to move for fear, the manager watched Davy go to the forge and spear a piece of burning coal. He returned, holding the flame well away from him, before plunging both burning coal and pitchfork into the pile of dry hay.

Whereupon, the terrified butler suddenly leapt out and, taking to his heels, made for the house, and safety.

Davy turned to smile at the farm manager, who was now convinced that Davy was a devil's disciple. The shaking man was holding out a one-pound note from the cash he had collected at the fair. He asked Davy to take it, to go away, in the name of God, and to leave them all alone.

Davy did so and turned towards home and his father and brother once more, for he was tired of the road and wanted to settle down on his own place. It was high time.

He was calmer in himself, and he had a pound in his pocket.

God was good.

5

NOT GONE AND
NOT FORGOTTEN

There was a woman in Limerick who was to be publicly hanged in that county who fled to Wicklow for the protection of Barrington of Murrough, a wealthy man of the powerful Barrington family. But her journey was to no avail.

For one reason or another, she had killed her husband, with the intention of marrying a particular young man. It was said that she hoped her influence with Barrington of Murrough would shield her and so she set of to his place on the coast of Wicklow, intending to stay there until the danger had passed, which in her foolishness she thought it would.

But her travels across the country were in vain, for her crime had scandalised the nation. She was arrested, tried and condemned. The date of the public execution was fixed and that was that.

But, some days before she was to depart this life in a most conspicuous way, she sent for the young man of her heart's desire. He went to see her in prison, though he'd had no hand in the murder of her husband.

If he expected remorse or lamentation for the place in which she found herself, he was very much mistaken. The condemned woman very coolly told the object of her attraction that she would come to marry him on November Eve: Hallowe'en.

The law took its course and she was duly taken out to be hanged before the local populace, as a warning to others not to transgress in a similar manner.

Determined to the last, it was said that she paid the greatest attention to her dress and how she would appear in public, for the last time. She walked to the gallows wearing a pair of fashionable brogues with silver buckles that caught the light and tapped out a step as she made her journey from one world to another.

Though she was dead, she would never rest. In the days following her execution, she still managed to upset the senses of the young man on whom she had set her sights while still alive.

It was not long before neighbours remarked that when the young man went out at night for his evening stroll the sound of those silver-buckled brogues was heard on the road beside him as he went on his solitary way.

Thus it may be supposed that the young man did not look forward to the final day of October with particularly joyful anticipation. Reports say he dressed himself very carefully in the evening, as if in anticipation of some very important and exciting moment. The evening wore on towards midnight and, to the horror of his friends and family, the sound of brisk brogues came to the door. Like one enraptured, the young man broke away from his sister and brother and his friends, and left their company. They reported later that they heard the steps of two persons fading in the distance, until all was quiet once more in the dark night.

Next day, the young man was found drowned in the nearby river.

The echoing footsteps were heard no more, nor as far as is known did the spirit of the hanged woman return to her hiding place in Wicklow.

Wicklow abounds with stories of the dead and of their return to this world if matters did not go well with them on their departure.

The well-known walker J.B. Malone recounted a story of a man who was buried in the turf-banks in Kilcoagh, in the west of the county. Before the potato famine had devastated the country, the said man – a Donard man named Lynch – had murdered his wife, and promptly disappeared. It wasn't known why he killed her, but he did.

There being no family to plan a wake for the dead woman, the neighbours did so, in the woman's own house. Candles were lit about the place, but come the witching hour of midnight, the horrified watchers saw the candles around the corpse suddenly quenched, as if by an invisible hand.

Needless to say, there was consternation in the sudden darkness. Someone lit a taper from the fire in the kitchen and the candlelight flickered to life once more as they relit each candle in turn.

A search was made at once, both inside and outside the wake house, in case it was a prankster intent on frightening the pious and the overly susceptible.

The sudden and unexpected death of the unfortunate woman was bad enough, but tragedy followed tragedy when they found the body of her husband, Lynch, hanging from a beam in an outhouse. He had taken the life of his wife and then taken his own.

It was a sin to take the life of anyone, or so it said in the Ten Commandments. At that time, a suicide was considered to have died in sin, for he had taken his own life. It followed that the person who took their own life did not have time to be shriven of their final mortal sin.

This complicated the matter of burial in consecrated ground, as in normal circumstances only those who were thought to have died without sin could be buried there.

So, the good people who were attending to the burials of Lynch and his wife had a problem. With the light of the candles restored and prayers said for her soul, Mrs Lynch was buried in the graveyard with ceremony and prayer for the peaceful rest of her immortal soul.

The next problem was how to dispose of the coffin in which the suicide lay. It was buried somewhere or another, as was convenient; but imagine the astonishment of the decent people who knew both deceased parties on discovering the coffin back in Donard the following morning. They buried it again; but whenever an interment was made, the coffin would return with the body of the wife killer and suicide inside it.

In the end, they made no further attempt to bury the confused man in either consecrated or unconsecrated ground. The coffin was put down below the surface somewhere in the turf-banks of

Kilcoagh, where it has ever since remained, according to local lore. Though that may not be the end of the matter, for it is a fact that the bog protects and preserves some things, especially wood, and the man was buried in a wooden coffin. Perhaps the last has not yet been heard of Lynch. Who knows what the bog may give up, in its own good time?

The playwright John Millington Synge came across a Wicklow story from the nineteenth century that has echoes in other parts of the country, where it seems that people in official positions were all too happy to declare someone dead, even if the grim reaper had not yet arrived to collect them.

He said he had met a man at the top of a long hill (of which there are many in Wicklow). Damp clouds hug the mountains of Wicklow three days out of five, and on three days out of five they bring rain to the hills.

On this particular day, Synge met an old man with a white, pointed face, who told him a story. They spoke first about the broken weather, and then the misfortunes that had been witnessed in Ireland. The man recalled the blight that came in the year 1846. Up to then, potatoes had been clean and good; but that morning a mist rose up out of the sea and you could hear a voice talking nearly a mile off across the stillness of the earth, said the man.

This continued in the following days until people saw the tops of the potato stalks collapse as if the life was gone out of them. That was the start of the failure of the potato crop. The famine devastated the country; but even when it was over, a cholera epidemic followed on, in 1849, and killed many of the famine survivors, already weakened by starvation and fever.

Mandatory reporting was the order of the day and when the wife of a man called Michael took ill he reported it to the authorities. She was duly taken away to the sick-house, and he heard nothing more till he was told she was dead, and was to be buried the following morning.

At that time, sufferers would be brought in during the collapse stage of the disease, when it appeared there was no pulse extant. Such was the fear on every person not to be in contact with the condition that they buried people they had no hope for, even if they still had life within them. At least, that is according to the old man on the top of the mountain pass in Wicklow, who claimed knowledge of such things.

Michael, wishing to be sure that his wife was indeed lifeless before she was buried in the ground, went down in the darkness of the night into the dead-house, where they had put his wife.

There were more than fifty bodies in there, lying among the shadows. All was still and quiet. There was no movement any-where, except for the breath rasping in and out of Michael's mouth. Not knowing what to do, he went along feeling from one body to the other to see if he could meet with the familiar form of his wife.

It may be supposed that his wife heard him coming in the dark-ness, for she wasn't dead at all.

In which case, she said: 'Is that Michael?'

He said it was, and asked if she had her last gasps in her still.

She replied that she had. She told him they had laid her out with fifty other bodies, so they could put her down into her grave at dawn.

Michael asked if she had the strength left in her to hold on to his back if he lifted her up.

She replied that she had, surely.

He then took his wife on his back and carried her out by lanes and tracks till he got to their own house once more. She was not missed from the dead house. Michael said nothing at all to anyone about what had happened, or what he had done.

At the end of three days his wife began to improve and, in a month's time, to the astonishment of her neighbours and the entire town, she began walking about again, just like her old self.

For all that the townsfolk were glad to see her back from the dead, there were many people who were afraid to speak to her, for they thought she had returned from the grave. And that was too strange an occurrence for many people. So they nodded at her and passed on in silence, the same as if they had met a ghost on the road.

6

A SHOWER
OF STONES

When motorised transport was a thing of the future and the bicycle had yet to make its way into Irish culture, a man was going to Rathdangan in Co. Wicklow to play cards and to see his friends. He was on a road he had traversed many times before. He knew where the houses were along the way and knew which of them were empty and which of them were occupied by mortals, and which by another presence. So he was more than interested when he saw a bright light not far before him where a bright light should not ordinarily be. Initially he thought it a trick of the light or the reflection of something that had been thrown into a field by a man passing along, who had perhaps tired of his burden. Nonetheless, he kept on walking by the edge of the road, just in case it was a carriage coming along in the darkness.

The elusive light came closer and at length passed him by. It passed back again and kept passing him until he reached Rathdangan. He saw no more of it after that, and thought it wise to say nothing to his companions for the evening, lest they think him fanciful.

Many hours later, and with a few cups of tea inside him and the heat of the house around his person, he left for the return journey.

This time he encountered no light along the way, but he did pass a big house with a slated roof. Slates were a matter of note at the time, as houses were usually thatched with whatever came to hand that was up to the job.

He paused to study the building. He thought perhaps it had stood there for a long time but had been surrounded by tall green trees, now suddenly gone astray, and that was why he hadn't seen it before.

Then he saw a long white shape laid out in front of him in the form of a coffin. It was not something he was expecting to see, and he had heard nothing himself of a recent death. Someone in the house he had just left would surely have mentioned it, if that was the case, for word of mouth spread faster in those days than any newspaper could hope to match.

He was perplexed and thought it might be an empty coffin fallen from a coffin-maker's cart on the way to some distant parish where a wake had been announced. If so, people would return for it, for a corpse without a coffin will not make a proper funeral. He walked to the other end of the box to see if there was a name on it, so that he could enquire further.

But, try as he might, he could not get to the head of the coffin, for it was taken up without him reaching out a hand to touch it. It moved along a little and was placed out in front of him, as before.

Matters proceeded thus, the white coffin kept moving in front of him, until he came to a lane leading into a bog. Then the coffin disappeared.

He walked on, keeping a sharp eye for any sign of a coffin or the shape of one, or an owner seeking a similarly shaped wooden box. But he never saw it again after that night. Nor, for that matter, when he walked the road to Rathdangan once more did he ever come across the slated roof that had appeared beside the spectral coffin.

In time, he wondered if it had ever happened, or was it just a mist that he had encountered on the low-lying road? And was the slated house, when he had looked up at it in the dark, nothing more than a steep bank with fanciful shadows on it? He did not know, but repeated the story to a few people he thought might make sense of a moving light, a large dark house, and a coffin that vanished into a bog.

Some say it was a signal from a person buried unofficially in that particular bog, but nothing has come of it so far; no body has turned up in the bog, yet. Nor a moving coffin either. Though something might still happen, for time moves slowly in the hills of Wicklow.

Another such tale would have been known to the people who used the graveyard of Kilranelagh, situated about 7km or so outside Baltinglass, which is about 14km from Rathdangan, for those who walk between those places. A story collected by Patrick Kennedy in his 1891 work *Legendary Fictions of the Irish Celts* concerns the graveyard and how a trickster was himself made to vacate his hiding place in somewhat of a hurry.

Most burial grounds are surrounded by a wall or a ditch thrown up to create a private space inside for the deceased and their mourning relatives and friends. At the time at which Kennedy reported the following story, the boundary wall at Kilranelagh was formed of loose stones piled one on top of another. The top of the wall was narrow in comparison with its base. Every man attending a funeral there brought a stone that he picked up on his way, and placed it on the circular stone fence. In consequence, with every stone placed, the ring of rocks grew higher.

One time, two men were returning to their homes in the gathering twilight, with a quickening step. They decided they would take a short cut through Kilranelagh graveyard.

They made their way up the hill, and were about to pass through the cemetery, when they heard the most awful groans and frightful outcries. And then, a shower of what seemed like cinders from a fire fell on them. Looking about, they saw that it appeared to be emanating from the direction of a tomb just on their left. Without debate or consultation, they retreated down to lower ground.

But, the further the pair proceeded away from danger, the braver they became. After getting to some distance away, the two men paused, plucked up courage and returned to the graveyard, even if their steps were a little slower this time.

However, if they thought that a second venture would be more uneventful than the first, they were mistaken; for they were met in a more fearful fashion this time, and once again fled in terror, tumbling down the now familiar escape route.

Nevertheless, few Wicklow men like to be bested by something they have not seen with their own eyes. As in all good stories, Kennedy reported that the pair made a third attempt at gaining the graveyard, unaccountable as their sally might appear to a more reasoning mind.

This time, they took two steps forward for every one step backwards, in an elaborate show of defiance and diffidence rolled into one. Both were poised for fight or flight, whichever seemed the best option. But if they thought they had the besting of whatever it was, they were mistaken. The noise was more appalling than ever, and a terrible being, with a wild cry, sprang up from behind the monument and rushed at them in the gathering darkness.

Down the now-familiar hill the two men flew like the untamed deer of the nearby hills. After a wild, unchecked flight they took breathless refuge in the first cabin they reached, where the occupants listened to their distraught story with not a little nervousness.

And that was the story of the two men who fled from the unknown in Kilranelagh graveyard. However, Kennedy, ever the story collector, offered an alternative version, as collected by him from the fiend of the tomb.

For the fiend was none other than a young man whose family owned a nearby farm.

As is the way with idle youth, few opportunities for devilment were left untried by this lad. He later related the story to Kennedy of how he was seated on the stony wall that enclosed the graveyard, when he saw, in the dimness of early evening, the two men making their way uphill on their way to their shortcut through the graveyard.

He at once conceived the idea of frightening them with a strange voice and with something flying at them through the air. He placed himself behind a large table-tomb and gathered up a pile of small stones loosened from a recent burial. He tossed the stones in an arc to ensure they rattled down in as wide a pattern as possible, while not actually harming the fleeing men.

The strange and frightening noises they heard came from his throat and consisted of the howlings he contrived to make in the darkness.

He admitted his surprise that the two men had returned to challenge their fear not just once, but a second and a third time. By their third sally he had been running low on stones and was becoming concerned at being unmasked if they came any closer. He was glad, therefore, when they gave up the ghost and finally fled downhill and away from the faux fiend of Kilranelagh graveyard.

But that was not the end of the story; for just as the men's third attempt at gaining the tomb had been abandoned, he himself was startled by a rustling sound among the dry weeds and stones behind him.

Something in the men's fear had been contagious and the jester soon found himself in headlong charge through the gloom, as a result of his own panic.

What was chasing him was never revealed. Maybe it was something that was in his own mind. Maybe it was a third party to the tomfoolery that went on in the graveyard. Or perhaps something else had answered the wild cries of humans as they chased themselves out of the graveyard and away from the company of the recent dead.

7

MOVING
ABOUT

There was once a man who used to go from house to house in the Glen of Imaal. He had no permanent home and seemed not to be any the worse for it. He had one thing in common with most of the people who travelled the roads at the time, and that was a fear of the Union, an official home for old and infirm tramps and tinkers. It was looked on with horror by most people. It was even more disliked than the madhouse, where many a person was detained often for no more than a bout of depression at the wrong time.

From 1838 onwards, a system of workhouses operated under the Irish Poor Law Commissioners. A stigma attached to workhouses meant they were perceived as providing charity for the shameless, the idle and the shiftless. Ending their days in the Union poorhouse was something most wanderers tried to evade.

Most people, no matter who they are, will generally have some liking for a spot at which to be buried. It might be a graveyard with a view, or a family plot selected long ago by a dead forebear. It might even be that they would like their ashes sprinkled somewhere special.

According to a story recalled in the 1930s by Mrs Tyrell, at that time in her forty-third year and living near Knockananna, Co. Wicklow, within sight of Keadeen Mountain, a wandering man left an amount of money with a family to bury him, whenever the time came for his soul to wander off to some other world.

His time of passing came upon him without warning as he died suddenly in a field, or so the story goes. And while he had left instructions with the family on what to do with his remains, those who had the job of dealing with his dead body did not know about this arrangement, and so his remains were taken to the county home that was in Shillelagh at the time.

After the legalities of registering his death were concluded, he was interred locally and most people thought no more about it beyond a few who remembered him in their daily prayers, for a while.

However, his soul had always been restless, and would not be calmed or lie easy. Some time after his burial he appeared to the people with whom he had left the money, as a reminder that the capital was given to them for an express purpose. If that purpose was not followed then it did not follow that the funds were to be retained by that family for their own purpose.

It was said that the oldest man in the family was so frightened by the whole business that he died soon afterwards, though if he thought he would avoid the travelling man he was mistaken, for all he had done by dying was to join the other lad on the far side of the great mystery.

The family members, in their sorrow and confusion, asked some neighbours to go with them to Shillelagh to exhume the remains of the unquiet man. They did so in broad daylight, with enough prayers said that would rise the entire population of the graveyard. Then off they went with the remains to the man's chosen burial ground in Ballymacrow in the parish of Killiskey. We are not given the man's name in the story as told by Mrs Tyrell, so we don't know which of the deceased sleeps there with more content than the others; but one thing is sure, the family who saw to his burial never had a bit of trouble with him afterwards, from that day to this.

He was laid to rest and was content to stay there; unlike another man in a different part of Wicklow, who almost frightened the life out of a pair of cattle drovers one early morning, while on their way to market.

In the early part of the twentieth century, fairs were only held in big towns and cities and so buyers and sellers had to go there to transact business and to trade livestock. At that time, the large trucks that carry all sorts of animals to fairs and markets throughout the country were not yet available.

Many people prepared their selling stock for days beforehand, gathering them in and making sure they looked their best for the sales ring. The journeys were by road and either the owner, or hired-in drovers, shepherded the animals on the hoof along the roads to the market. And since markets always take place in the early hours of morning, so as to allow time for an onward journey by the buyer, those people who lived far away from the sales area started the journey at night in order to be there by dawn.

To complicate matters further, it was said that restless spirits were abroad until cockcrow. Spirits were expected to leave the world when the cock crowed, at which time the world was safe for mortals to move through once more. Many people delayed their journey's start until the cock heralded a new day.

In a story told by 62-year-old John Stanley Smith of Moyne to 11-year-old primary school student Noel O Briain, two men were going to a large market town with a drove of cattle. It must have been high summer for they arose at 2 a.m., ate a full breakfast, checked the stock and decided that once the cock had crowed a blessing on their journey they could be away about their business. So it was that they headed out, confident enough that they would secure a good stand for their animals when they arrived at market.

They were an hour or so out on the road when they heard horse's hooves hurrying towards them from the rear. Jocularity was suspended for a while as they moved aside to make room for the approaching rider, as was custom and practice.

With fierce shouts and a great whacking of ash plants, they cleared the cattle to one side of the road for the rider and horse. They stood to one side with some interest in what was causing the rider to approach at such speed. He was surely on a mission, such was his haste, and the two men wondered what it could be to cause such a rush.

As the rider approached, they thought they recognised his frame astride the horse; yet he did not slow his pace: he merely shouted that he had no time to speak to them and must keep moving.

He rode on out of sight. The drumming of the horse's hooves faded into the distance as the quiet sounds of morning surged back once more.

The drovers exchanged a few names to try to work out who the rider had been. They went back to their schooldays in memory but it was no use; neither could truthfully say who he was or why he had passed by in such a whirl of hurrying air and dust. As they spoke, they hunted the cattle back onto the road, concentrating on the task in hand to make up the time lost by the disruption of the mysterious man on the horse.

Not long afterwards, in fact only about five minutes later (as they estimated in retrospect), they heard a terrible roaring like the sound of an angry bull coming up behind them, from the exact direction that the horseman had first approached.

This time, they drove the cattle under a road bridge for safety, for while little harm could come to their charges from an approaching horse they were unsure what to expect from the swelling noise that grew louder as they hurried the cattle off the road.

Whatever the roaring might have come from, it passed over the bridge and was soon fading into the distance, just as the sound of the galloping horse had done before it; they later believed that the horse's rider had been fleeing from the roaring noise that seemed to be in pursuit.

While one of the drovers kept the disturbed stock in place, as best he could, his companion looked out from beneath the bridge and scrambled onto the roadway for better observation.

He called out to his companion below that all he could see was a man progressing at high speed away from them. Of the horse and rider he could see nothing.

Both men knew well a story that Julia Doyle from Ballgobbin told of Patrick Furlong of Rathdangan, who was a noted runner who travelled long journeys on foot. Once, it was said, he started from Rathdangan to a football match in Rathdrum and ran most of the way, a distance of more than 32km, longer than a marathon, to see the teams play. He overtook a horse and trap in Greenane, so the story went. The driver, looking down at him, invited him to take a lift. He thanked the driver for the offer but said he was in a hurry. Patrick Furlong ran off, leaving the horse and cart behind him as it toiled along up the hill to Rathdrum.

Nonetheless, the drovers agreed that it was not Patrick Furlong who had been running along the road. For one thing, Patrick would have hailed them, civilly enough, as he passed, even if he didn't stop.

They gave up wondering about what had gone before them and bent to their task of getting the cattle back onto the road and heading in the right direction, in an orderly manner.

Two or three miles later on in their journey they came to a graveyard and prepared to cross themselves as they walked past, saying a silent prayer for the repose of the souls therein. To their surprise, they saw the horseman standing on his own two feet, praying like a mad monk with hands clasped and eyes closed.

Under the circumstances they could not walk on, and paused where they were, awaiting developments.

The man came out of the graveyard to speak to the drovers. 'I was your friend', he said to them, and they could just about remember a young lad they had known for a while one summer long ago.

'When I passed you on the road, the Devil was after me', he continued. 'I died with a lot of sins on my soul. But rather than be consigned to hell straight away I was given the chance of running around my parish at night. I was allowed to use a horse, if I chose to do so. If I reach a graveyard by dawn I will be safe', he added.

Whether he was mad, right enough, or had been saved from the Devil chasing him at speed down through the glen, was something the men would have to consider on their way home from the market, and with a few hot whiskeys inside them. For now, they were content that the horseman was dismounted, seemingly at peace and saying his few prayers.

The running bellowing figure was nowhere to be seen and the light in the sky was growing stronger. They drove on without looking back too much, for such is the life of a Wicklow drover, never sure what he would meet on the way to market of an early morning.

All that mattered to most was that he get there on time, running Devil or no running Devil, before the buyers were gone.

8

WISE MAN
PADDY STEVENS

As far as is known, Nasreddin Hodja, a thirteenth-century story-teller who lived in Aksehir in south-central Turkey, was never near Kiltegan in west Co. Wicklow in his life, or thereafter, as far as any credible records show. Nevertheless, a number of stories were collected in the Kiltegan area in the mid-1930s that have a similarity to the type of story attributed to Nasreddin.

Suspicious readers might wonder if the establishment of St Patrick's Missionary Society, otherwise known as the Kiltegan Fathers, in their first headquarters near Kiltegan in March 1930 had anything to do with it.

John Hughes, a tea merchant, gave an old house and 20 acres of land to the priests as a base in Ireland. Kiltegan became a retreat in which the diocesan priests working in Nigeria could spend their holidays. Who knows what stories found their way into local lore?

Did returning missionaries retell tales they had heard somewhere in Africa on their missions? And did the stories then congregate around the head of one Paddy Stevens, a local man who worked for a parish priest in the early 1900s?

We don't know what the priest's name was, but it was enough for local storytelling that he was the parish priest, a position of some importance in Irish society of the time.

On this occasion, the good man had somehow lost a cow of which he was particularly fond. He summoned Paddy Stevens and tasked him with finding the lost animal, and as soon as possible.

Paddy went out of the parochial house to begin his search and though he searched high and low he returned empty handed, or at least cow-less. There was no sign of the beast.

He assured the priest, with some earnestness, that he had searched in all likely places and the cow was not be found in any of them. The exasperated cleric suggested to Paddy that, in that case, he go and look in all the unlikely places that he could think of.

Imagine then the priest's surprise when he stared out of his window half an hour later to see the same Paddy Stevens on the roof of a nearby thatched cottage. He was standing precariously on the ridge and poking at the thatch, with some interest.

The priest donned his long black coat and official hat to go out to speak to his worker. On questioning him as to why he was up on a roof of a house that was not his own property, he received the reasonable reply from Paddy:

'You told me to look in all the unlikely place, but I can't find her here either.'

The response of the put-upon priest was not recorded. We can only imagine his feelings and his difficulty in maintaining dignity at having lost his cow and then having to engage in conversation with a man in his employ who seemed to have lost his senses.

Whether the cow ever returned, was located, or whether it emigrated to another parish or was rustled by someone else entirely, we are not told; the point of the story being Paddy's earnest prosecution of his allotted task.

A short while later, the parish priest was conducting religious instruction classes in a local school. He put the eternal question to one boy as to where God might be found. However, the boy had no clue at all where God might be found on a Monday morning. In exasperation, the priest suggested the boy leave the classroom and find someone who did know the answer, and to return with his new-found knowledge.

Of all people, the boy met Paddy Stevens outside the school. The priest had said he was to ask someone who would know where God was to be found. So he put the question to Paddy.

Paddy thought for a while and then gave the boy the answer he required. The happy youngster duly returned to the classroom and informed the priest that he now knew where God was to be found. He was in Keane's Barn, said the boy in triumph.

This was so obviously a parroting of another's response that the priest questioned the boy on the origin of his information and soon found that the source was Paddy Stevens.

He lost no time in tracking down the said Paddy, who expressed surprise at the priest's unease. The clergyman asked him why he had told the lad that God was in Keane's Barn. To which Paddy replied, quite reasonably, that if God was everywhere as the parish priest told everyone who would listen to him, then God might as well be in Keane's Barn if the young lad wanted a place to start looking for him. It was a point of religion that the priest found hard to argue with, despite his best efforts.

There was a growing conviction in Paddy that he knew as much about a great many things as the parish priest did. This conviction caused him to adopt an unusual regime when washing the priest's side-car, one of Paddy's regular chores.

To the priest's bemusement he arrived one day at his side-car, in readiness for his weekly visits to the sick and dying in the surrounding hills, to find that only one side of the side-car was bright and shining, while the other wore last week's mud with pride.

He went in search of Paddy, who was busy slicking down his hair with some water from an outside tap and a gap-toothed comb in preparation for driving the priest around the houses.

The priest asked, with some restraint, why one side of the car was cleaned but the other side was not. He also noted that the clean side was the side where the priest himself usually sat.

Paddy nodded in appreciation of the priest's perspicacity. He was quite right in his observation, he said, in a tone that made the man of religion wonder if Paddy had been drinking secretly.

But why is one side clean and the other side not? asked the priest in a measured tone.

'Well,' said Paddy, 'if I were to clean both sides of the side-car equally no one would know which of them was the priest's side.'

It was a concept that left the good man stuck for suitable words with which to respond. So he resolved to say as little as possible to Paddy Stevens lest there be any opportunity offered for misunderstanding.

However, this proved to be a drawback, when on another day he asked Paddy to saddle his horse for him so he could ride over to another parish to consult with a colleague.

He dressed well for the journey and stepped out into the yard to be off on his trip. Imagine his surprise, then, to find the saddle was fixed back to front on the horse's back.

Controlling his impatience, he went looking for Paddy to seek an explanation.

Paddy told the priest that as he had stopped speaking to him over the side-car incident, Paddy was at a loss as to know what the priest wanted when he asked for the horse to be saddled.

'But you saddled the horse backwards,' said the priest.

'That was because you didn't tell me which direction that you wished to go in', said a triumphant Paddy.

The unfortunate priest was almost at the end of his tether when a parishioner asked if she could borrow Paddy for some days to do some work around her farmhouse. The woman had lost her husband a year earlier and so was a widow woman (to use the parlance of the time).

Paddy duly arrived and set to work on his allotted tasks. It was made all the simpler by the priest briefing the woman before Paddy arrived as to how to lay out the work so that it made sense to Paddy's creative imagination.

All went well until it came time for a midday meal and the woman produced chicken soup for his nourishment. She left him to it and enquired, some time later, if he had enjoyed the soup.

He nodded and thought for a moment before asking what class of soup it might be. On hearing the proud boast that it was chicken soup, he replied that the chicken soup was so weak that the bird must have flown through it.

The widow, not wishing to appear ungrateful for receiving help with her tasks, asked Paddy if he would like an egg to eat.

To which Paddy replied: 'Begob, Mam, I knew a man that ate two and lived after it.'

Meanwhile, during the time that Paddy was away from his home base, the priest took a stroll along the nearby watercourse. And if he thought Paddy Stevens was the only strange man in the parish, then he was in for enlightenment.

For he met a man standing in the flowing water with a wheel in his hand. He was turning the wheel around to direct the flow of the water, while chanting an incantation to himself and the water. As far as the priest could make out, it went like this: 'All for me; none to Martin Doody. All for me; none for Martin Doody.'

Whoever Martin Doody might be was a mystery to the good clergyman, who had suddenly had enough of fools. He moved quietly to where the man was by now kneeling on the bank of the river, leaning over it with his wheel. The priest drew back his foot and kicked the man in the seat of his pants, sending him sailing into the water.

'There's something for you, and none for Martin Doody', he said with unsaintly relish.

It was a small transgression for a man who knew in his bones that he was going to have to live with the mad Paddy Stevens for a long time to come.

9

WARRING
SPIRITS

Two men went to war over religious belief in the early 1800s in the Kiltegan area of Co. Wicklow in a dispute that extended beyond the grave for both of them.

John Duffy was a Catholic and a servant in the home of a man called Kenna, whose first name we do not know. We do know that Kenna was from a family of Protestants. Not only that, but his whole family were Orangemen, a secret society founded in Northern Ireland in 1795 to maintain the political and religious ascendancy of Protestants.

Kenna and Duffy bickered a great deal about religion, about which of them was right and which was likely to see its adherents condemned to hell for all time, and a day besides.

As both men grew older, the arguing grew so bad and so heavy that Kenna's sons kept Duffy away from the company of their father. Duffy retained his job and was not dismissed; but he was prohibited from engaging Kenna in conversation about anything at all, though most specifically about religion, or on the subject of right or wrong.

While such arguments might seem puzzling to a modern mind, it should be remembered that Catholic Emancipation measures were not signed into law by George IV until 1829, some years after both combatants went to their respective graves. Before that time, many restrictions were placed on Catholics in their daily lives because of their beliefs, and advantages conferred on Protestants for belonging to the religion in power.

And if Duffy ever essayed the satirical rhyme about the Protestant King George IV: 'Georgie Porgie, pudding and pie, kissed the girls and made them cry. When the boys came out to play, Georgie Porgie ran away', we can only imagine Kenna's reaction at the slight.

The protagonists fought their way to a standstill, until the rising generation put paid to expression of passionate and opposing positions. So, it was a strange thing to hear that a declining Kenna had sent for Duffy to come to see him on his deathbed. Duffy went out of politeness and respect for an adversary, even if that person was his employer.

Kenna surprised Duffy by asking to see him in private, instructing his family to leave them alone for a short while so that they might discuss a matter of some importance. The family left them to it with some trepidation, for the last thing they wanted was to see their father engage in a futile argument over religion while on his deathbed.

If Kenna had surprised Duffy with the request to see him, he surprised him even more with his second request: for he told Duffy that he wanted to speak to a Catholic priest before he faced his final journey. He gave Duffy £20 and asked if he would go to Baltinglass and fetch the priest, leaving no doubt in Duffy's mind that Kenna wanted to convert to Catholicism before he died.

Duffy took the money, but to his shame, did not go to fetch the priest. Instead, he allowed Kenna to pass away without his final wish being met. His family were unaware of his last aspiration, the request having been entrusted to Duffy alone. But, Duffy was to pay for the consequences of his refusal and the stealing of Kenna's money.

Kenna was laid to rest at Talbotstown in 1820. But Kenna had unfinished business to attend to and was only twenty-four hours laid down when he returned and started to throw balls of burning clay at a somewhat startled Duffy, who thought it was all over and he was the winner. And a rich one at that.

Kenna continued to pelt the hapless Duffy, who, falling back on the support of his religion, sought sanctuary in Talbotstown church. It was to no avail, for the spirit of Kenna would not be rested without satisfaction. The throwing of missiles continued.

The priests of the parish moved to lay the spirit of the dead Protestant to rest so that the living Catholic could find peace. According to folklore, in the laying of Kenna's spirit, some 10,000 people are said to have attended at the church. It would appear that this was a highly unlikely figure and more than a trifle overstated, but given that onlookers apparently climbed up ladders and took the slates off the roof of the church to peer in at proceedings, who is to say how many souls were assembled on that day to bear witness?

The parish priest, Fr Gahan, the senior cleric of the parish at the time, commenced the prayers of reconciliation for the troubled spirit in what he hoped was a determined manner, given such a vast congregation, gathered if not in faith then at least in curiosity.

However, good intentions are not always sufficient to carry the day. As he progressed through the prayers, the priest entirely lost his faith in the proceedings whilst trying to lay the spirit.

This would have been catastrophe enough for anyone, but was pure disaster for a priest of some authority, standing in front of thousands of gawping county men and women. It was a fortunate thing that Fr O'Reilly of Rathvilly was there as an observer and assistant to Fr Gahan. O'Reilly was by all accounts an astute man. When he saw his colleague starting to wobble in his belief, O'Reilly moved to take his place.

Sensibly, Fr O'Reilly thought to ask the spirit of Kenna to state why he had returned from the dead and what he wanted of Duffy and, by extension, what he wanted of them as his religious advisers.

The spirit of Kenna revealed to the enquiring cleric that while alive he had given Duffy £20 to give to the priest in Baltinglass as payment to come to him as he faded from life. He then revealed that Duffy had advised him that if he said an act of contrition, he would be saved from the fate that awaited every Protestant in the next life, for their heresy.

A collective intake of breath greeted this revelation and public sympathy turned away from the pelted and tormented Duffy to the poor confused soul of Kenna, the man who had seen the light before his death and had asked to be allowed to be blessed by a minister from an opposing religion before he departed on his final journey.

Fr O'Reilly prayed quietly for the soul of the unfortunate Kenna, while a confused Fr Gahan looked on. The assembled hordes answered the Latin responses by rote, responses which if they did not quite understand them at least comforted the living in their recitation.

When all was over and Kenna quietened down, Duffy was banished from the parish, the £20 having been acquired from him by a resurgent Fr Gahan before he departed to pursue other interests elsewhere.

Such was Duffy's notoriety and the disapproval of his fellow parishioners that he moved away as far as Co. Kilkenny, where he passed the rest of his days exiled from his native Glen of Imaal.

Duffy may have repented his actions, but memories linger long for such a crime as to deny a dying man a last wish. Duffy's own dying wish was that he would be brought back to Cranerin cemetery at Rathdangan to be buried. Wicklow people went to meet his coffin as it came to the Glen.

In derision for his behaviour, the burial party planted him in the opposite direction to his specified wishes, echoing the injustice visited upon Kenna.

But if Kenna returned from the dead in spirit, so too did Duffy. For he visited the two principal gravediggers that very night, not even waiting the twenty-four hours that Kenna had taken before making up his mind to return.

Duffy terrorised the two men, who while they were happy to disregard a dead man's wishes were not quite up to engaging in battle with the risen Duffy.

When he appeared to the two men they were enjoying a bottle of mountain dew after their exertions. They were rehashing the entire saga from the arguments of the two living men through the death of a repentant heretic to the denial of Duffy's dying wish.

Duffy was from the Glen of Imaal and he insisted to the startled men that he would be buried as custom dictated – as everyone else in the Glen would be, in turn.

The distraught men took their picks and shovels to the grave-yard early the following day and dug up the coffin of the dead Duffy. They reburied it in the approved direction and shovelled the clay back in, with some haste, then departed.

The story might be expected to end there. But according to local storytellers the entire family of Kennas, who were Protestant and Orange to a man and woman, turned Catholic after that. Though whether that was from religious belief or a desire to confound everyone else in the spirit of their dead father is hard to tell. Perhaps the ructions between Kenna and Duffy continued on in the after-life, and Kenna was up to mischief through his kith and kin.

Who knows what might happen when two men begin to argue over who is more right than the other man?

In this life, or the next.

10

TAKEN BY
THE FAIRIES

An old man lived in a townland in Glenphilipine, Co. Wicklow, at some time towards the start of the last century. It was when most people in a family had a given name for official purposes and a local name to separate them from others of the same family. This man was known as Murtagh the Coiner, though at this remove we do not know what the reason was for his nickname. He was an unmarried man, never having heard the call to depart from his solitary status as a bachelor.

However, according to a story collected in the 1930s by Bridie Hanley of Tinahely, from Michael Needham, 45, of Ballyshanogue, Tinahely, the Coiner was one day crossing a ditch with a harrow on his back when he fell down, heavily.

A harrow, as everyone knows, is an implement for breaking up and smoothing out the surface of the soil. He was not badly injured in the fall but he was winded and his head was a little dizzy, as an old man might be from suffering a sudden and profound tumble, when he least expected it. He decided, therefore, that he might as well stay where he was for a while, to allow his body to adjust to its changed perpendicularity. When all was calm once more, he would arise and continue on with his business.

Acknowledging to himself that he was alive and would arise in a moment when matters settled themselves inside his skull, he allowed that the fall could have been more serious than it was and could indeed have been fatal.

He could have been killed. He acknowledged that fact and then said to himself, 'I could have been killed without knowing the good of a woman.' Other people might have thought of other things, but that was what the Coiner contemplated while lying there on the ground.

Sometimes, a single moment changes the trajectory of our lives. It was no different for the Coiner, who after rising from the ditch and finishing his harrowing went in search of a wife, in contradiction of his long-held bachelor philosophy.

According to Michael Needham, who told this story long ago, the Coiner married three times after that. We can but hope that he enjoyed some good with one, or all three, of his wives before he lay down himself for a final rest.

At a different time, Mollie Mason, who lived in Aughrim, told of another story of a sudden change, this time in the lives of a married couple of the county, a change that came about through no desire or action of theirs.

The wife of Larry Wolohan, a farmer in Ballycoogue, was taken one summer evening by the fairies. This may seem astonishing to a modern mind, but it used to happen a bit more in older days than it does now.

As might be expected, Larry Wolohan spent all evening searching for his wife, whom we shall have to call Mrs Larry, for Mollie Mason did not supply her name, as was the custom of storytellers in the olden days. It was enough to say that she was a missing wife.

No matter where he looked, Wolohan could not find any trace of his wife. In the end, he gave her up for lost, though he asked his neighbours to continue to keep an eye out for a stray wife.

Then, one night it happened that he was coming home late from a fair when, to his surprise, he saw a little man sitting on a gate ahead of him. As he approached, the man hailed him and they started talking, and it was not long before the diminutive person gave him some advice on retrieving his wife from the fairies.

He told Larry to be on the hill above his house the next night at midnight, and he would see his wife riding past on a white horse. The man told Larry that when she passed him by he was to grab her and hold on to her. He was not to mind what the others would say to him and on no account was he take his eyes off his beloved wife.

Naturally enough, Larry Wolohan agreed to do just that; but, nevertheless, he went to seek advice from the local priest, his spiritual adviser, whom he supposed had some insight into the other world, as well as this one.

The priest advised Larry to go to where he was bid, for no harm could come to him if he had his rosary beads with him. He was to make sure he took the beads with him. For good measure, the priest blessed the beads in Larry's hands, and away went Larry to await midnight on the hill and a joyful reunion.

Sure enough, at the appointed time, he saw his wife coming through the gap between a pair of fields with the fairies in front of her. She saw Larry, with some relief, and called to him to catch her as she passed, which he did. However, the accompanying fairies shouted at Larry to look around to see what was behind him.

Now, although he had been instructed not to take his eyes off his wife during this time, such was his quite natural human exultation that he looked away for a moment. Needless to say, there was damn all there; to make matters worse, when he looked back again his wife was gone, as were the fairies, and the white horse she had appeared upon on the hill.

From that day onwards Larry Wolohan never saw his wife again, no matter how many midnights he passed on the hill above Aughrim.

To say the fairies were gone would be incorrect, for they manifested themselves in different ways even if they remained invisible to mortals. But, like mortals, they enjoy a touch of mischief every now and then.

In another tale, which took place a good way through the last century, the grandmother of a local woman, Mrs Whelan, at that time in her forty-third year, was coming home one fine evening from visiting a hillside household in Aughavannagh. The *fear an tí* (the man of the house) came down to the foot of the hill with her.

They stood talking for a moment before parting at the foot of the lane, near the Union Cross. Things were going pleasantly enough when the man was hit around his head by something resembling a whip. He was surprised, for there was no one there other than Mrs Whelan and himself.

'Why did you hit me?' the man asked.

'I did not hit you at all', she replied, in some puzzlement, as she had seen his cap move as if struck by an invisible force, but she was at a loss to explain it, no more than he was himself.

It did not happen again and they parted company as civilly as possible, for they were neighbours living deep in the Wicklow Mountains and did not want any unpleasantness to remain between them.

According to the story, that same man was killed in an accident going home from a fair a short while after that. It was said by some people that it was the fairies that did it, but no reason or evidence was ever advanced to prove the case.

Another man who was said to have been taken by the fairies in the same general area of Co. Wicklow was Mick Byrne. In 1937,

Mrs Byrne of Tinahely told Gladys Roache of Killaduff House, Aughrim, the following story, which is preserved in the schools folklore collection in Dublin.

Mick Byrne was going home from evening prayers at his parish church, located on the way to Macreddin, to the west of Aughrim. He was accompanied by some friends with whom he was exchanging banter to shorten the road.

Just beyond the Tinker's Gate he was taken, quite unexpectedly, from beside his friends by some force that was as unexpected as it was invisible and powerful. The unfortunate man, eventually left on Donnelly's Brow, was in his senses if a little confused when he realised where he was – alone and without his friends of a moment ago.

Country people were well schooled in the way of 'the other crowd' and tended to live and let live, but it seemed on this occasion that mischief was afoot and that poor Mick Byrne, for some unknown reason, was to be the butt of it.

Now, any field that you might encounter in any county in Ireland will have a gate in it if it is adjacent to the road, or a gap to pass through into the next enclosure if it is an internal field. Nonetheless, no matter how many times Mick wandered around the field he had been left in, he could not find a way to get out of it.

He took off his long overcoat and turned his coat inside out before putting it back on once more, to see if that would show him the way.

It did not.

He sat down and removed his boots and threadbare socks to see if that would show him the way out of his predicament.

It did not.

So he began to shout to see if that would make a difference.

It did, for Tom Donnelly, who lived nearby, heard him calling in the darkness. Tom thought the voice sounded familiar. He fetched a lantern from his house and went across to where the shout had come from in the night.

He was astonished to find poor Mick half-dead under a bush, exhausted from his frantic efforts to free himself.

Tom brought the distressed man to his own house, where he gave him strong tea with white sugar in it for the shock and a drop of poitín for good measure to put a bit of fire back into the mortal body.

When Mick recovered his voice and his composure, he assured the Donnelly family that he had been taken by the fairies and deposited on Donnelly's Brow without his permission or any foreknowledge at all. Tom Donnelly and his eldest son walked Mick to his own place and made sure he was safe and well and tucked up in his bed before turning for home themselves.

But they took two lanterns with them to light the way, for who knew how you might go astray on a dark night in the Wicklow Mountains, when mischief was about.

11

A FLEETING
BIRD

Long ago, people used to wander the roads of Ireland from one end of the year to the other. Some families were disrupted by famine evictions and were still wandering a few generations later. Some were people who had fallen out with their own families and had left the hearth to wander wherever their fancy took them. Some were returned from travels abroad in the army or navy or in search of a personal fortune that did not come their way.

More than 100 years ago, John Millington Synge observed that tramps in Ireland were little troubled by the laws that others abided by, and lived in out-of-door conditions that kept them in good humour and fine bodily health. This was so apparent, in Wicklow at least, according to Synge, that these men rarely sought charity on any plea of ill-health, but asked simply, when begging of others: 'Would you help a poor fellow along the road?'

Perhaps we can assume, then, that such travellers of the road were skilled in storytelling to get along. One man, who died at the beginning of the twentieth century, claimed to have reached 102 years of age. Synge recalled that several old people remembered the man's first appearance in a certain district as a man of middle age, about the year of the famine, in 1847 or 1848, so it might have been true, or maybe he'd had an older brother who resembled him. Who knows?

The tramp claimed that in his early life he had spent thirty years at sea. When he was too old to face any more oceans, he learned all the paths of Wicklow, and till the end of his life claimed he could travel the 50km south from Dublin city to the Seven Churches of Glendalough without putting out his foot on a white road, or seeing any Christian, but only the hares and the moon.

When this voyager was aged more than 90 he married a younger woman of 85 years of age. Sadly, they had more years than sense between them and they quarrelled so fiercely that he beat her with his stick and returned to the roads. However, whether he believed himself subject to the law or not, within a few hours he was arrested on her complaint, and sentenced to a month in Kilmainham Gaol in Dublin.

If the dampness of an autumn evening on the hills of Wicklow was kept at bay by the stone walls of the prison, so too was the comforting sound of a cow chewing the cud in the heavy shadow of a bush. He did not hear the echoing bark of a pair of dogs calling to one another in their own language on the side of a hill, or the yelp of a frightened deer in flight up a steep incline, or the rumbling of a cart upon the white stony road in the distance.

The tramp cared nothing for the plank-bed and uncompromising diet presented to him as prison hospitality; but ever afterwards he cursed with rage when he recalled how his gaolers cut off the white hair that had grown down upon his shoulders through the years.

Synge observed that all the man's pride and feeling for the dignity of age seemed to have set itself on this long hair, which marked him out from the other people of his district, as indeed it would, for he would have had the appearance of a prophet, or at least a man wise enough to be consulted on matters of importance.

But, tramp or no tramp, he was unwise enough to be jailed for the beating of his wife with a stick over a marital disagreement, which had led the law to come looking for him.

Yet at least his wife had been alive when her husband left her. She was able to report him to the Royal Irish Constabulary, who set out on his trail. There was a more serious incident a few years later, in the Aughavannagh area. Or at least that was where it ended up – where it started is anyone's guess.

At that time there were two particular people who went around the countryside together and it was supposed they were man and wife, though they referred to themselves simply as 'himself', or 'herself', so no one knew what their relationship was. Perhaps they were siblings grown too old to part from one another.

Then, one day, the woman vanished as surely as if she had taken to the high road and had struck out for Kilkenny, or Carlow, or south to Wexford or Dublin to the north. When anyone asked the man where 'herself' was these days he shook his head slightly as if he didn't want to talk about it, or even contemplate life without his companion of the roads.

After a while, his visits to certain touchstones became less frequent and people began to forget when they had seen him last, or when he was due to call once more. Eaten bread is soon forgotten, they say, and as time went by the couple were both forgotten by most people.

Other news began to occupy conversations in the glens. One story was told of a poor fellow who was reaping all day in the lower field. In the evening, he had two glasses of whiskey with some other lads. Now, some people can drink whiskey until the cows come home and others cannot. The reaper was one of the latter. When the last drop of the second glass arrived inside his skull some excitement took him, and he threw off his clothes and ran away into the hills as naked as the day he had first seen those same hills.

A great rain came down that night, and it was supposed by the recovering constables that the demented man had lost his way in the dampness and darkness and that his body was not up to the task of keeping itself alive until sense returned to the man's mind.

The next morning, concerned neighbours found his naked footmarks on mud half a mile above the road, and again further up on a sheep path by a big stone. Search as they might, there was nothing known of him until he was discovered a few days later, stone dead on the hillside untouched by carrion crows or any other living scavenger.

Another such story was related for the schools folklore collection in the 1930s by Laurence Whelan, who had been told the tale by his father of the same name. One day, two boys were going to the same hill with sheep to leave up there to graze so that the lower areas could have a chance to grow back. As is the way with young lads, they took all day to do a job that should have been only a few hours in duration. Once the sheep were safely led onto new grazing, one of the boys produced a few cigarettes he had stolen from home and the other produced a solitary match to light the first cigarette.

Having only one match meant they had to light a fresh smoke from the declining butt of the previous one. So they smoked just one cigarette at a time, passing it to one another after each puff.

After a while, one was as dizzy as the other, and no matter how much they spat saliva from their mouths onto the red clay and shining rocks, a taste lingered that made their stomachs feel unwell enough to make them decide to head downhill towards home.

There are a number of road bridges crossing tumbling water in the area and all natural-born boys linger at every one to drop sticks or throw stones into the passing water. It is a ritual of the ages, taken up by all small boys and occasionally indulged in once more by the same boys when grown to maturity, if few are watching.

These two particular boys were crossing a stone bridge after conducting a race of twigs in swirling water, when on one side of the road ahead of them they saw a lovely bird. It was a bird whose breed they did not recognise and so, being boys, they decided they would catch it and take it home as a trophy of their day on the hill. Besides, they could account for any missing hours, or neglected chores, by claiming that the hunt for the fine bird had taken up their time. All would be forgotten in the wonder of the coloured feathers of their trophy.

In true boy-hunter fashion, each went either side of the road and advanced on the balls of their feet with suppressed breath, and contained excitement. The bird watched their approach with a stillness that caused more disquiet between the hunters than their approach seemed to cause to their prey.

Once upon their prey, the lad with the cigarettes grabbed the head of the bird and the other, the single-match man, grabbed the feet.

Their triumph in capture quickly turned to bewilderment, for they soon found that they were holding the head and feet of a woman and not the bird they had stalked with such determination. Naturally enough, the two boys got the biggest fright of their lives.

They released their captive, certain that they wanted no more of it. Letting go of all physical contact, they jumped away as far as they could. They gazed at the extraordinary transformation of a fleeting bird into a human woman who seemed to carry the sorrow of the glens on her shoulders and in her face.

The boys ran all the way home, no matter the distance. All tobacco sickness was forgotten as they ran and paused for breath and paused once more, hands on knees, as they looked to the road behind them to see that they were not being followed by bird or woman.

On their arrival, the excitement of the boys drew a similar response from the people of the area who soon enough set out in a party to see what the hubbub was about. For although the purloining of the cigarettes had been observed – and small boys under the

influence of their first cigarettes have been known to become dizzy – seasoned veterans of life knew, however, that there was more to their experience than a few puffs on a hillside can explain.

On reaching the spot near the bridge, the boys pointed to the woman on the road. Their companions may have been sceptical of the boys' story, but no adult thought it wise to approach the woman too closely.

One of the party declared that it was the woman of the pair known as 'himself' and 'herself' who had not been seen in ages. Once identified, the others agreed it was her, surely.

Nonetheless, they stayed their distance until the woman pointed at a shore beside the road near the stream that passed beneath the bridge, from where the lads had recently thrown their conquering sticks down into eddying waters.

Two men stepped forward to see what she was pointing at. It was not long before they pulled away gorse and lank overgrown grass to reveal a firmly placed flat stone in the soft ground. While all eyes were on the stone and the exertions of the two strong men, the woman vanished out of sight, never to be seen in earthly or avian form again.

The murdered body of the woman was discovered under the stone. It appeared she had suffered head injuries from a stick. The police and a priest were called to remove and pray for the dead woman and a hunt was put up for her male companion.

It is said that the shore for many years afterwards was called the dead woman's shore.

For her, there was no more roaming to be done. For the man who killed her, justice was in pursuit.

12

THE LONG WALK TO CROIS ÚNA

It is always wise to make arrangements for your own funeral before you die. Failing that, a noncombatant member of the family should be entrusted with the task, lest the coffin go astray on the way to the grave.

A good many years ago, a woman who resided with her only brother in Glenmalure died of one thing or another and was waked at home, as was the way.

The house was cold and they could not afford glass for the window. Instead, two sticks were crossed and a kid's skin nailed across it. This was repeated in the other window, leaving the inside of the house very dark as light travels very poorly through goatskin. The only light was that which came in over the half-door.

People commiserated with the woman's old bachelor brother, who was unsure as to who was shaking his hand at any given time. His sister had expressed a wish to be buried in a particular graveyard where other family members had been buried over the years. She was a practical woman and had left a small purse to cover the expense of her removal and burial.

And so it was that a number of local men of impecunious means agreed to undertake the journey with the remains inside the coffin.

The first thing they decided was that they would carry the coffin on their shoulders. That way, they would save the cost of hiring a horse-drawn hearse. And therein lay the problem, for they had forgotten that a funeral will stop at a crossroads to say prayers for the departed, and there were a great many crossing of pathways on the way to the burial place. That is, if you were to count every boreen that intersected with the clay road they started on at the beginning of the journey.

For a while, all six stood with caps removed and heads bowed and said a sorrowful decade of the rosary before hoisting the coffin aloft once more. The woman had been a slip of a thing and weighed less than nothing, and the coffin was the cheapest money could buy; but the constant marching in close proximity to each other and bearing a weight upon the shoulders drew out whatever strength they had brought to the task.

After a while, common sense prevailed. One would say the prayer in a respectful stance and the others would take their ease on the grass while making the responses out loud. It was early autumn at that time, when the bracken had turned and there was nothing much to be heard in the countryside, save for the buzzing of a few late bees and the autumn song of thrushes. It was a peaceful class of a funeral with no wailing keeners to distract the six men from their reflections. The heavenly landscape told them that the soul of the deceased was in heaven. It imbued their work here on earth with a pious purpose. Each halt took longer, until it became apparent that if they continued at this rate they would never get there at all.

They decided they would rule out boreen crossroads as bona fide prayer stops. This they did while standing around the coffin. They looked down at the lid of the casket as if awaiting a sign from the deceased as to her wishes. No answer came, so they hoisted up the morsel of weight once more and stepped out with a little more determination. Now that they were off the mountain tracks they would soon come to some establishment or other where they could slake their thirst on this warm autumnal day.

Before they went too much further, they turned off the road and laid the coffin in some long sedgy grass, with due reverence. They placed their hats on the lid and settled down to eating a few cuts of bread they had brought with them for the journey.

It was the custom of the time to have two meals, one in the middle of the day and an earlier breakfast of potatoes, porridge and buttermilk. People usually worked for the first hour before breaking from work for a breakfast. The men made short work of the bread now that the middle of the day had arrived. They each had a brace of corked bottles of stout in their pockets, kept over from the wake. These they opened with full solemnity to wash down the crumbs of soda bread that lingered on their lips.

After that, they dozed for a little while, secure in the knowledge that they could not be seen from the passing road and that no one could accuse them of frivolous irreverence to their client's memory.

They were men of the hills and their slumber lasted only as long as was appropriate: one stirred, they all stirred. The journey recommenced. Looking at the sky and the sun's position, and knowing with the mountain man's sureness exactly where they were and how far they had to go, they knew that the interment could not occur before darkness landed on them. The burial would be tomorrow, they knew that now; but they had no way of sending on word to the officiating priest that they were unavoidably delayed on account of saying too many prayers on the way.

They had a vague idea that this would prove a valid excuse for not fulfilling their end of the bargain – to get the remains to the graveyard for burial on the same day. They were men of the hills and close to the secret mystery of things, which said that for every action there was a reaction; for every wrong there was a righting.

But they were puzzled as to whether that extended to saying too many prayers while the corpse was in your company and missing a burial because of it. They soldiered on for the time being, stepping along as smartly as any flying column would do in the hills on the way to an ambush. They said very little to one another. The prayers at crossroads were delivered with a swifter response than heretofore and they were off again. In this way they covered quite a deal of the journey without losing much more time.

No more than anyone else, they were not able to slow the passage of the sun across the sky, nor slow the clock as it raced through the daylight hours remaining. The best they hoped for now was a late arrival on the same calendar day. So long as midnight had not passed when they got there, they considered they would arrive on the day appointed, even if a nightime burial was out of the question.

However, they came then to the crossroads at Ballycarrigeen that was known as Crois Úna, where a shebeen operated. A shebeen was a place to meet and discuss political and social issues and to consume unlicensed alcohol. A range of home-made drinks were available in most shebeens, as in this one.

The bearers laid down the coffin in a field behind the shebeen for a prayer at the crossroads. They needed a drink, but drew the line at bringing the coffin into the shebeen, so they placed their hats on top of the coffin, to show that it was not unaccompanied, and entered the shebeen.

One drink called for another. The day drew in around the coffin outside while the men inside spent their day's earnings on another drink or so. They drank everyone's health and more besides and began to feel cosy within.

What with one thing and another it grew so late that they decided, in their wisdom, to go home, leave the coffin at this point on the journey and to return on the morrow to take up their burden once more. It was the reasoning of the inebriated and none questioned it.

However, they could not leave the coffin and the remains of the good woman exposed to the elements until they returned. So, they piled a great mound of rocks around it so it could not be seen by anyone. Well satisfied with their work, they wandered home retracing their own footsteps.

Now, great intentions often get lost in the mist of time, and a few drinks can cause collective amnesia. It happened that the select six never returned to complete the funeral procession. Perhaps they forgot, perhaps only some of them were available on one day, and not on another, and time passed while they waited for a day that suited them all. It never came, and the good woman remained entombed inside the mound of stones, sleeping away like a pharaoh of another time.

Since the men had not told anyone in the shebeen of the purpose of their journey, no one thought to ask why there was a mound of rocks in the field, where there had been none the day before.

If anyone remarked on it they might have thought that the Good People were up to something or other. In any case, no one went near the mound of rocks for a long time afterwards.

That is, until Bill Hawkins, a servant of Hugh Byrne of Ballycarrigeen was sent to draw stones from it to build a drain, many, many, years later when the shebeen was gone and the six bearers had come to dust in their own time.

Bill started to pick out the stones he thought would best suit the work in hand. He had a few likely ones laid out on the grass for onward transportation and was content with his efforts. Then, to his astonishment, his reaching hand withdrew a bone from inside the mound. He was not long about legging it home to his employer, after that, to say he would go no more into that field to draw stones.

There was something inside that mound that should not be disturbed, he said.

And so the pile of stones remained where the six bearers had left them.

They may be there yet.

13

Milk
Profit

Revenue generated from milking was known to a family as their profit. In one particular case, the cows of a particular man in the glen of Aughavannagh in the south of Wicklow stopped milking, for no apparent reason, and profit dried up – a serious matter at any time.

The farmer tried all techniques known to him and his neighbours, but nothing would resolve the problem. Nonetheless, when there is a problem someone will offer a solution or suggest a remedy and so it was in this case, according to local man Laurence Whelan who heard the story from his father of the same name.

The family called in a qualified man to restore their profit for them. They related their difficulties to him. He listened well and nodded and said he would take on the task. What was more, he would start that very night.

When the family retired to bed, the man of the house stayed up with the profit retriever to see how his profit was to be returned. The house fell silent, as one after the other the humans nodded off to sleep. The man asked the farmer to turn down all the lights in the house, the better to be able to see what was happening in the darkened yard outside.

All was quiet until, as midnight chimed, the two men heard a noise in the yard other than the normal foostering and scootering that emanates from farmyards. Both peered out through the small windows of the darkened room.

The man nodded, while the farmer stared and stared but could see nothing more than what was customary.

Seeing his confusion, the man asked the farmer if he ever saw the fairies who lived nearby. The man had to say that he had heard enough stories about them and was aware of the pishogues associated with fairies, but to date he had not had personal contact or dealings with 'the other crowd'.

The man told the farmer to look out into the yard, in that case. When he did so, he was startled to see that a massive change had taken place. For where he had gazed out at an empty space before, he now could not see the ground for fairies trooping about the place.

The man stepped back from the window and closed the curtains. He had asked the farmer to keep the fire glowing. He now stepped over to the hearth and placed some irons he had brought with him into the fire among the glowing embers. He explained to the farmer that the warmer the irons became, the warmer the person who had taken the profit would get. And they would soon see what had happened to the profit from the cows.

They stood and watched the irons glow redder and redder and waited. Not much time had passed when the latch was lifted and someone came in. It was a small woman hunched over and in distress. She was hot and bothered and was engaged in pulling her clothing from one side to another to encourage cooler air to circulate around her submerged skin.

She stopped short of the fire and the red-hot irons that lay there. She looked from the fire to the man, and the farmer knew then that she was the cause of his problems with the cows and his stolen profit.

The woman asked the man if he would take the irons out of the fire. He did not do so at first, but instead he studied her long and hard. When he did not shrink from her staring gaze, she asked him again to remove the irons from the fire. He nodded, but failed to move one inch towards the fire. On her third appeal, he stepped away from her to draw the irons away from the heat. He placed them to the side in the cooled ashes, where they gradually faded from burning red and back to quiet black as they cooled.

The woman said no more to the man, but as the heat declined she seemed to gather strength from the cooling of the metal, however that could be. She left the farmhouse once more, saying nothing at all to the farmer as she left.

As she departed, the hired man sat down as one who has had a weight lifted from his shoulders. Work done, the farmer joined his wife in bed and the profit retriever slept through the night on a settle bed beside the glowing embers of the once-hot fire. When daylight touched the room once more, he arose and left.

That day, the farmer brought in the cattle for milking with some interest and not a little doubt for he was ashamed to think, even for a moment, that he might have had a trick played on him by the man and the small woman. They might have had him pay to have his profit restored when it had simply dried up of natural causes.

However, he was pleasantly surprised to discover that milk was flowing once more from his animals. As time passed, he noticed an even stranger thing: from that day on, the cows gave more milk than they ever had before the profit was taken from them.

Yet he never saw the woman again so he could not ask her how that could have come about. It was a mystery.

In another part of the same glen, a large farmer lived with his wife and family on a snug farm. According to Patrick Redmond of Knockanooher, who recalled this particular story, the farmer was very rich and had a lot of land on which he kept horses and cattle. In fact, the farmer's enterprise was so extensive that he kept two workmen to assist him and a servant girl in the house to look after domestic chores. As was the way, the girl was sent in the evenings to bring the young calves into the yard to feed them.

This she did with a cheerful step, for it meant she was out of the house and away from any supervision that might be visited upon her indoors. She was generally able to lead the calves along the way to the yard by waving her arms about and making clucking noises with her tongue. But, about this time, her charges were growing bigger and friskier and she decided on this particular evening that she needed a stick with which she could tap the recalcitrant ones on the rump to make sure they went the right way.

So, in all innocence, she pulled a stick from the top of the ditch at the back of the house and off she went to where the calves were half-waiting her arrival. That evening, they were no trouble and kept ahead of her along the lane to the farmyard where, for a change, they turned in themselves, every one without exception.

The larches in the haggard were dripping heavily with damp from the evening rain, every leaf and twig was heavy with drops of moisture. Domestic hens and geese cackled in the yard with more than usual dread. Even the pigs seemed restless and moved away to a far corner. The girl's senses should have been disturbed.

But, paying as little attention to such things as the young ever do, she turned into the yard and closed the gate behind her to make sure that no animal ran away while she was tending to her charges. She was not long at her task when the farmer came out to see that all was well, having been disturbed by the cackling of fowl and the scratching and bunching up of the pigs. He stopped short when he saw the stick on the ground.

'Where did you get that stick?' he asked, with a touch of trepidation in his voice that the servant girl had not heard him use before.

She told him its origin and for good measure took him to the spot where she had broken it from the bush that grew there.

'Do you not know that the hedge at the back of this ditch belongs to the fairies?' he asked her. 'And that stick too?'

The girl had not known this. But, there and then she fell down in a faint at what she had done. The farmer took her into the house and laid her down, before hurrying off to Aughrim to fetch a priest. The clergyman came as quickly as he could, but his ministrations were to no avail. The farmer also sought assistance from others besides the priest, but in vain. Despite what anyone could do for the girl, she faded away and died. The poor girl had passed away over a simple mistake.

She was buried quietly and with some sorrow for she was known as a girl who was always ready with a quip and a laugh as she passed through life.

All were sorrowful in the days that followed. In time, a new girl came from Glenmalure to take her place in the house and to take up the girl's duties. Imagine, then, the consternation caused in the house when the new girl asked who the girl sitting up on the ditch might be, she who never returned a greeting but who was always there while the calves were being brought in.

The farmer went with the new girl on the next evening to see for himself. He knew just who it would be that he would see there. A dense white mist had rolled down from the hills and normal everyday landmarks rose up from the mist when least expected. Every block of white stone seemed to be the size of a small dwelling, every concourse of water seemed to have the determination of a Nile just beginning its epic journey. It was easy to believe you saw something you should not have seen, or to miss a turning into a lane and walk on for miles on end, to no purpose.

The mist cleared and there sat the dead girl, quietly watching all that passed. The farmer told the new girl not to be afraid, but to pass on about her business whenever she met the other girl, without speaking to her. Every night for a long time, the lost girl appeared sitting on the ditch holding in her hand the stick that had caused all the trouble.

But she caused no trouble and the farmer left her there without seeking to have prayers or incantations said to remove her; for she had paid a high enough price for picking up one single stick that belonged to 'the other crowd', without knowing at the time what she had done.

Perhaps she sits there still.

14

A Cure for
Baldness

Judy was a Murrough girl who married Davy Brian, a thatcher, and took to the roads of Wicklow with him to follow his itinerant craft. The coastal wetland of the Murrough extends for about 15km along the coast from Newtownmountkennedy down to the pier at Wicklow harbour, but the pair soon moved into the hills where most of the work was to be found. A thatch lasted in best condition for about four years on a house, so there was always some thatching work to be had in the glens.

Judy's father had outlawed her for marrying Davy, for he didn't think much of him as a son-in-law or as a provider for his daughter. However, Davy was happy enough with Judy, and she with him, and they got along well enough. Davy swore she brought him money in a dowry, but no one ever saw much sign of it in the time that followed.

In any case, Davy was a well-known liar who liked nothing so much after a day's work but to sit down with fellow travelling tradesmen to swap lies and tell tall stories. So well did he tell his tales that the house he was in used to fill up with people anxious to hear lies told about impossible situations in which Davy allegedly found himself.

He told a story one night of a walking-woman he met who had a cure for baldness. Now, it was a curious fact that bald heads were not to be seen that much in the countryside. It was not that they were not there, it was that they were hidden under the hats or caps that everyone wore, since long ago, in the outdoors. The only way to know if a man was bald was to attend the same church as him and to see what happened when he removed his cap on the way into worship. For males were not allowed to have their heads covered at Mass, while women were not allowed to have their heads uncovered at Mass, such were the mysteries of religious observance in Ireland at one time.

And because the men wore caps or hats all week while the Wicklow weather beat into their faces and gave them a permanently tanned appearance, their little round skulls were as white as their behinds on the day they were born, for no sun ever shone on them. Some deniers trained stray strands of hair to go from one side of the skull to the other in the vain hope that people would not notice the arid desert over which it travelled. They were fooling no one but themselves.

Even so, few others had the gaucheness to remark on hairdos that vanished under headgear as soon as the outside air was encountered, once the celebrant had blessed everyone and told them to go away in peace, for now.

On this particular night, a wandering schoolmaster who went by the name of Mr Saul, or Fr Saul, was staying in the same house as Davy and Judy. He might have been a priest left over from the days when the saying of Mass was prohibited, though that seemed unlikely given that prohibition had been done away with from 1829 or thereabouts and Davy was explaining this cure for baldness some 100 years later.

The man might have been a failed priest who at one time was in the full flow of a vocation but became a civilian once more, now taken to wandering the roads teaching reading, writing, prayers, Latin and history for a living as he passed along.

When he was not teaching he worked as a casual labourer in the fields. There were others besides the tradesmen who tramped the same roads. Labouring men who hired themselves out, as required, were known as spalpeens, though if you were to call such a man by that name you were likely in the early stages of a clash that might leave you badly injured or with something loose inside you that shouldn't be so.

Workers in wood were known as hedge-carpenters and they walked the roads as well. They made everything from chairs to sit on, to the wooden spokes of a cart, though such jobs would often take seven days to complete and they were paid 2s 6d (a half-crown) per day. There were eight half-crowns to a pound in the old money and these were hard to come by, as everyone knew. The weekly wage for a herd on Powerscourt Demesne at that time was twelve shillings for a week's work; there were twenty shillings to a pound.

On this storytelling night, while Davy was accepting a small libation from the man of the house, he allowed the floor to go to Saul.

In honour of Judy, Davy's wife, Saul recalled that the Vikings founded towns at Waterford and smaller communities at Arklow, and Wicklow, as well. Many exotic goods were brought into Ireland from Britain and Europe, he said. Shipbuilding was also an important industry along the coast, as you might imagine, he said, for wooden boats could be built on a sloping shore and pushed into the sea as soon as they were ready to float away.

There were many benefits for people living in the countryside near these new seaside towns. The inhabitants of these new towns needed food to eat, and timber to make houses and ships. Farmers who lived in the hinterland were only too glad to supply the townspeople with food and timber, he added, as if he had some personal knowledge of their relationships.

He did not mention whether or not the same Vikings, whose credo it was to take what they wanted at any time, actually paid for goods received or simply accepted such things as tribute from a frightened populace.

'It was the old walking-women that brought the knowledge of such things around the country', interrupted the now lubricated Davy, to take the story away from his wife's people and forebears, for there was no way of knowing if any fraternisation between the races had occurred. He did not care to dwell on the possibility that Judy's father might be some part Viking and might now be sharpening an axe on the way to searching for his daughter on the high roads of Wicklow.

The schoolteacher was nonplussed; he didn't know whether Davy was agreeing with him or suggesting that his talk was woman's talk, or whether he was being challenging for superiority.

He made the mistake of pausing for clarification and that was the end of him, for Davy was away with the cure for baldness that he had heard from a woman of the roads down near Greenane one winter's night long ago. It was her contention that women did not go bald, for a good reason.

Davy asked if any of the company had ever seen a bald woman. He asked in the same way you might enquire if anyone had heard a banshee calling for them. People were only too happy to shake their heads and affirm that they had never seen nor heard tell of anyone who had ever seen a bald woman.

Davy explained that this was as a result of headgear.

'Women,' he said, in the manner of a well-travelled man who had made a study of baldness, 'wore hats that were a fit for the shape and size of their heads, whereas men wore hats that would stay on in a gale from the sea or a storm in the mountains, or both.'

This was a practical matter, for a man could not spend his days pursuing hats and caps all over the place when he was working. That was to the detriment of a fine harvest of hair upon the head, Davy said.

People now looked to Tom Cullen in the corner, who had only known hair on the crown of his head for a few short years before he went prematurely and permanently bald, as did all the men in his family. They looked to his cloth cap, which even now in the heat of the indoors of the cottage was as firmly ensconced on his head as were his flaming eyebrows over his rheumy eyes.

But Tom said nothing as he wondered to himself when he had last worn a cap loose enough to let the breeze from the soft bog cross his scalp. He couldn't remember when that might have been, but he asked the thatcher what he was getting at, so he could arrive at a conclusion by which he could measure his own baldness. Perhaps, on the days when he was alone on the hill with the sheep, he might leave the cap off and see if any hair would grow on his bare head.

'Well', said Davy in a lowered voice that induced the listeners to lean in to listen with more attention to him. Even the wandering priest found himself turning his head so his ear could come closer to this piece of information. He would travel on tomorrow and if he had a cure for baldness he might give up teaching Latin grammar to wild Wicklow kids who'd rather be out on the hills than listening to him and his declensions. Curing baldness would probably be easier on the spirit.

Davy drew something from his pocket and showed it to the gathering crowd. Three straws sat side by side in the palm of his hand.

'A bald man need only to burn three straws like these and then rub the ashes in the bald place and hair will grow', he said, with the air of a man sharing the secret of serenity.

'Does he need to leave the cap off, so?' asked Tom Cullen.

'It would help, but it is not compulsory', said Davy as he stood up to throw the three straws into the fire, where they were instantly immolated with a sizzle and flair, to the bewilderment of the astonished watchers.

'It's a skill', said Davy. 'You need to watch out for the walking women and ask them for three such straws. From such a companion I learned that skill', he said as he prepared to retire for the night.

And not for the first, nor the last time in their life, did people study Judy and wonder if she was the fount of Davy's wisdom and storytelling abilities.

For who knew what abilities the Vikings had left with the people of the Murrough and the coast of Wicklow, where it faced the known world.

It was enough for the thatcher and his life's companion that they wondered at all.

15

Now You See It, Now You Don't

Two brothers went to England from Wicklow with cattle in a time when live cattle were exported from Ireland. They travelled in winter and were killed by a storm at sea when the ship, cargo, crew and passengers went down.

Before their voyage, as was common at the time, they stayed overnight on their journey at places that offered bed-and-breakfast accommodation for drovers, and space for animals on the move to feed and rest. That evening, back in Wicklow, the woman of the house they had last stayed in saw one of the brothers standing at the well. He said nothing, and when she looked away then looked back again his image had vanished.

Naturally enough, she was frightened at the sight, for word of tragedies at sea travelled slowly in those days and news had not yet reached their home county that the men had perished.

She told everyone she met what she had seen by the well. People put great store by apparitions and signs as indications to be taken notice of by all. And when word came that the brothers' vessel had sunk, interest rekindled in the appearance of the man at the well.

According to a story first told in October 1937 by Mrs C. Deeringage, 48, of Lemastown, Co. Wicklow, and held in the National Folklore Collection, the woman of the house, the *bean an tí*, went to the priest to see what she should do for the best.

The priest told her if she saw him again to ask the man what was troubling him, which she agreed to do and returned home.

In the early evening light, the man was there again at the well. She stepped out, making sure no one was around to observe the encounter, for she wanted to be clear about the torment that was keeping the man from peace.

He spoke to her in words that no other listening mortal could hear: it was more that she looked at him and knew what he wanted to say. He said he had died without doing penance for his sins. When she asked what she could do for him, he asked her to do penance for him.

She said she would and asked him what that penance should be.

He answered that she should travel to the church on her knees, saying prayers for his immortal soul on the way. To this she agreed and informed the priest that it was to happen. He agreed to be present at the door of the church when she arrived on her knees.

All went well and, as word spread of the penitential journey to the church, more and more people lined the route. Many joined in public prayer, making the journey almost as long as a pilgrimage.

The way was muddy in places and those people who followed the penitent put hay down for her so she could move along in a little more comfort.

But some invisible impediment existed and she found herself unable to proceed, try as she might, until the hay was removed. Once it had been taken up, she was able to carry on along her route to the church. The priest gave a public absolution for the sins of the sinner represented by the kneeling woman, whose dress and knees were now torn, and whose blood seeped from the grazes on her legs from the multiple vicissitudes encountered on the journey.

Once the final prayers were said, the ghost was not seen again.

In another part of Wicklow, the 77-year-old Laurence Whelan of Knocanoocra heard the following story from his father.

Long ago, there was no postal delivery to individual homes. Those that thought there might be post for them went to a post office in a designated post town and collected their messages from there.

Betty O'Toole was returning from collecting her post one day and as she was coming down Kavanagh's Hill, she saw a man coming up the same hill towards her. She thought she recognised the man as Pat Neill, who used to ramble to Kavanagh's every night, and she hoped he wouldn't delay her too much, for the lateness of the day was enveloping her.

She called out: 'Is that you Pat?' But no answer came from the approaching man, whose face was averted from her in such a way that she could not be sure who he was in reality. He passed by her in silence.

Her interest piqued by now, Betty followed after the man, at least for a few steps. If it was Pat she would have a word with him, and if it was not Pat she wondered what the man's intent was, for she knew by the hunch of his shoulders that he was about some business or another.

He stepped off the road where Tommy Byrne had left a few clamps of turf for collection. The man lit a small enough fire from the nearest clamp using a few cuts of furze for kindling. He soon had a steady fire going. Then the fire itself grew bigger and bigger until the flames were leaping up as high as the tallest man in the glen could stand.

A mesmerised Betty sat unobserved by the ditch as the fire burnt on through the night. Towards dawn, the fire grew smaller and Betty nodded off into a private slumber. When she awoke, the man had gone. But the turf was there still, undisturbed, it seemed.

She stepped into the empty field. No ashes were visible on the ground from the bonfire and when she looked at the clamps of turf they were intact to the last sod.

Betty O'Toole stepped back onto the road and resumed her journey, wondering all the while who the man might have been for he was no earthly man, of that she was sure.

When she next met Pat Neill she asked if it had been him, but he assured her that it had not. Thus it was that the man's identity remained a mystery to her for the rest of her life, and to anyone to whom she related the story. And there it was left, an intriguing tale with no explanation, as yet.

The 53-year-old James Tyrell of Rathshanmore, Wicklow, related a similar story of a man met upon the road who did not return a greeting.

A man was setting out for a fair, quite a distance away. His wife told him that he should be home early, before it grew too late. He replied: 'I'll be home, alive or dead.'

The day passed, night came and he did not return. His worried wife yoked the horse and cart to go and look for him, leaving an old lame man to mind the house while she was away.

Half a mile from home she met her husband on the road approaching her. He passed her by in silence.

The woman turned for home wondering what the matter was. On her return, the lame man told her that he had heard the door open a while earlier, just before she came home. He heard someone come in but he saw nothing.

Search as they might they could find no sign of the silent husband, or anyone else, in the house.

The next day, word came to them that the man had been taken ill on the road and died. So, he had kept his promise to return that night, alive or dead.

Another strange occurrence that happened in the dark of the night occurred at Killaduff, Aughrim. A man named Fred Roache first related the story, which he assured his listeners was true.

In the days when grave robbing and selling corpses for medical research was a profession of sorts, two robbers arrived at Annacurra cemetery on business.

One of them tied back the gate so they could drive the horse and cart in and out with ease in order to transport the resurrected corpse to an awaiting medic. They reopened a freshly filled grave without disturbing too much clay. Then they took the corpse out of the coffin by breaking the lid open close to the face of the deceased person and hauling them out with a rope around their neck.

That done, they rolled the body into a sack, swung it well between them and tossed it up on the cart. Then they drove the cart out of the graveyard and prepared to set off on their onward journey, a somewhat unexpected one for the poor soul behind them.

Once on the road they halted the cart and returned to the graveyard to fill in the grave once more, and to close the gate, so that no one would notice anything amiss.

However, unknown to them, they had already been observed in their work. A pair of watchers in the shadows cast by a graveyard tree had seen all. More than that, the men were relatives of the deceased, on guard for just such a raid by sack-'em-up robbers who plundered unwatched graves.

While the robbers were cleaning up at the graveside, the men moved to remove the corpse from the cart, with alacrity and reverence. They gently placed it a little way away to await reinterment, with a priest present to observe ecclesiastical niceties. One of them then climbed onto the cart to take the place of the dead body. He rolled a sack around himself and waited, quite still.

Soon after, the robbers jumped up on the cart and drove off, well pleased with their handiwork and the prospect of payment when delivery was effected.

Yet further along the road, while going over Onnacurra Bridge, one of the robbers thought he heard a moan from the corpse and reached back into the cart to place his hand on the body. He said to the other: 'Lad, the corpse is still hot!'

With that, the supposed corpse leaped up and said: 'If you were where I was for the last few days you'd be twice as hot.'

It's not every night that a dead person speaks to you. It's even rarer for that person to complain about the heat of the place he has been in; so it is of little surprise that the robbers jumped off the cart and ran away into the night, travelling in different directions at some speed, away from the resurrected corpse on the cart behind them.

That left the undead man with no option but to drive the cart home to his own place for retrieval by the owners, should they ever come calling for it, once his loved one was reburied.

It is not recorded that they ever did so.

16

SHRIVEN SOULS

In the line of observing religious practice, people from time to time come up with some strange notions of what is right and what is not right. At one time, long ago, it was frowned upon to play cards on the Sabbath, which was Sunday for most people in Ireland. Some said it was the Devil's work and others said it brought bad luck to play cards on Sundays. Others went around to the back of the ball alley, formed a standing circle of people, and played poker with a pile of cards on the ground between them. Such a practice was technically illegal as the law of the land at one time forbade such Sunday card games. On 12 January 1871, Andrew Carty was brought before the Avoca & Rathdrum Sessions, charged with a breach of the Sabbath by playing cards at Kirrakee, somewhere between Laragh and Glenmalure, in Co. Wicklow.

At other times, at the same sessions, people were charged with offences that we might not see in our courts in present times. In December 1869, Catherine Carty of Kilmagig was charged with damaging timbers and fences at Ballyarthur, the property of Colonel Bayley, on which land the game shooting was said by visiting gentry to be excellent.

In December 1900, James Doyle of Poulaphouca was charged by the Earl of Wicklow of poaching a rabbit from grounds being lawfully used for keeping rabbits at Ballinvalley, near the elusive gold fields of the eighteenth century. The unfortunate man was also charged with stealing one snare.

In 1870, Michael Doyle of the Meetings was charged with trapping rabbits, the property of one Charles Stewart Parnell of Avondale, as was Mary Doyle of Ballyteague, in the same year, charged by a representative of Charles Parnell Esq. with trespassing on Parnell land at Rathdrum and carrying away brushwood.

In September 1870, John Doyle of Cronebeg was charged with furiously driving a horse and cart through the street at Rathdrum, a street that later became famous when it was used as a location for a raucous public meeting and street fight between republicans and RIC in the film of the life of Michael Collins, the twentieth-century revolutionary.

Whether any of the accused went to confession in the church before they faced the court is lost to history; but there is a story told of a man and his son who travelled from Kilgowan to sell cabbages in Dunlavin one Saturday in 1897, according to Peter Grace, who got the story quite a few years later in November 1937 from T. Grace of Dunlavin – so the story is probably true if it lasted that long in local tradition. Or maybe not, for the Wicklow storyteller likes to spin a good yarn.

What happened, we are told, was this: the man and his son arrived in the village and noticed that confessions were being heard in Dunlavin church the following day, Sunday. The older man decided it would be a good idea to be shriven of his sins. He told the younger man to mind the cabbage while he stepped in to see the priest and have a chat with him, not that he needed to, he assured his son, but he would go in just in case he had overlooked something the last time, as you never knew with these things.

Once inside the quiet church, the man soon found the confession box, set into the side wall. There were a few people there ahead of him so he took the opportunity to sit and stretch his legs after the walk into Dunlavin with the cabbages.

After a time, during which he almost nodded off in the pew, it was his turn. This fact was notified to him by a loud cough from the bustling woman who was next in line beside him. According to the story told, his visit to the confessional was briefer than his sojourn on the church bench. The cabbage seller blessed himself and said: 'In the name of the Father and the Holy Ghost', after which he continued with the rest of the introduction of himself as a sinner, as was the custom. But he was soon stopped by the priest.

'Where do you leave the Son in the middle of the prayer?', asked the priest. 'It's in the name of the Father, the Son and the Holy Ghost', he said.

The man straightened up from his kneeling position, without quite standing up and said: 'I left out the son because he's outside on the road minding the cabbage until I come out, Father.'

It's rare enough for a confessor to refuse absolution to a penitent; but, on this occasion, the man was told in no uncertain terms to leave the confessional, the church, the parish and the village and to take his son and his cabbage with him. And what's more, the aroused priest promised he would be in touch with the curate in the man's home parish to inform him of the cabbage seller's transgressions in the church on this day.

What happened to the wandering cabbage seller after that is not known. But the tale of his attempt at enlivening the dreary recitation of human fallibility remains with us to this day. We can only imagine what might have happened when he arrived at the gates of Heaven to discuss his entry permit with the keeper of the gates, if he persisted in changing the format of address there too.

If that particular priest was a stickler for due process then another priest in a quieter part of Wicklow – according to Bartholomew Grace who collected the following story as part of the Schools Folklore Collection in 1930s Ireland – was more a man of the world, who took a broad view of human failings.

Two gentlemen, who had a fondness for spirits of another kind, decided it would be a good idea to make amends with the Creator for their ways. In some cultures these men would be described as a pair of drunks, but all that people said of them in Wicklow was that they were martyrs to the drink – drink being something that had happened to them just to afflict them with its seductive anaesthesia and confused reality.

Both had been away from confession for a long time when they happened down Main Street one fine Saturday evening, when people were gliding in and out of the church like bees at a hive in high summer. It could only be confession that was going on.

The two gentlemen spoke about it for a while, yet maintained a distance from the black church gates. They agreed it would be a marvellous idea. They would confess, one at a time, accept their penance and start a new life, on the best foot, that very evening.

However, as close as they were in drink, brothers in fact, they drew the line at going into the church together. So one found an unspent penny in a corner of a pocket and, before tossing the coin to decide who would go in first, they passed some time seriously considering which of them would be on heads and which on harps.

Once they had decided, the coin flew through the air and chose one of them. The first appointed stepped into the coolness of the church porch, paused and took a deep breath. Grasping the ornate door handle with determination, he stepped forwards onto the linoleum of the church floor. The door closed slowly behind him and all was silent. The second man watched the door with some interest, and perhaps not a little anxiety, for he was damned if he could remember a single sin he had committed in recent memory. He excluded the sin of drunkenness and gluttony from this examination as constituting a state of being rather than a considered and chosen way of hedonistic life.

He was running through a few white lies to tell the priest on the way to absolution when his boon companion came back out of the little church with a lift in his step. The newly blessed man had a beatific smile on his face that puzzled his pal of the road, who wondered what had happened. It was their personal and collective experience that clergy were inclined to give a man who was partial to the drink a rollicking in confession, the better to send him seeking the road to abstinence. That the latter seldom happened made no difference at all to the same zealous reforming clerics.

The second man caught up with the other gentleman after a few yards and a shambling run, which almost made him trip over his trailing second-hand overcoat that swept the dust off the road behind him as he went. He caught his friend by the sleeve to halt his progress. The man smiled at him and awaited a question. He was in a state of transportation of the spirit.

The unshriven man asked him how he had got on and why he was so happy in himself. The penitent smiled and said that the priest was a lovely man who he could speak to for a very long time.

This was the class of answer that any drunk would give to a benefactor who assisted him in the matter of a complimentary libation.

Again, the gentleman asked the other why he was so happy and what had happened in the confessional.

Again, he was told that the priest was a very nice man.

Puzzled by this, he asked how the confessor had reacted to the matter of over-fondness for drink, to put it mildly: 'What did he say about drink?'

'He never mentioned it, like a decent man, and nor did I say a word about it, since it never arose in the conversation. You could talk to him forever he is that nice. A great pity there aren't a lot of other priests of the same mind as him. They'd get a lot more business if they were, especially around Christmas time.'

It wasn't long before the second man was ensconced in the kneeling position in the darkened confession box, rattling off every venial sin he had ever encountered.

And his friend was correct: the matter of drink never came up in the chat at all. For which both men gave thanks as they wandered off down the road to their next watering hole to discuss this strange occurrence and to raise a glass to an understanding priest.

Some people have strange notions of what is right and what is not right in the line of religious practice. Perhaps the priest had seen more of the world than he let on to the two knights of the road who stepped into his church one fine Saturday evening.

Who knows?

17

WICKLOW
FOXES

Ghosts of times past may lurk about the lakes at Blessington and in particular at Poulaphouca, where the administrative boundary forms between the counties of Wicklow and neighbouring Kildare.

Twin valleys were flooded here in the 1940s to form a large reservoir for Dublin's water needs and a hydroelectric facility at Poulaphouca gorge. Dozens of farmhouses were covered with water once their inhabitants had been housed elsewhere to make way for the stored water that came to the reservoir off the sloping Wicklow hills. In times of drought the remains of some of these house are exposed to view.

Where the dam now stands tall, an unimpeded natural waterfall existed that was formed by the descent of the River Liffey through a narrow opening in a craggy precipice, falling from a height of upwards of 55m, over several progressive ledges of rocks, till it was precipitated into a dark abyss, where it formed a whirlpool of frightful appearance and immense depth.

According to Weston St John Joyce, writing in 1912 in his book *The Neighbourhood of Dublin*, it was considered to be the most picturesque fall in the county of Wicklow. A handsome bridge, of a single Gothic arch, soared across the chasm through which the water rushed. The span of this arch was 20m, and its keystone was 55m above the level of the river below. Sharp and naked rocks overhang the glen for some distance, both above and below the fall.

Poulaphouca means, in the old tongue, the home or hole of the Pooka or Púca. It is generally considered that on All Hallows' Eve, the dark and sullen Pooka is particularly mischievous. Many mortals are abducted to fairyland on this night against their will, with the connivance of the Pooka. Those persons taken away are sometimes seen once more at Hallowe'en by their living friends.

Children were told that the Pooka went about on this night spitting or urinating on all wild fruits, which were not to be eaten thenceforth. Indeed, the Pooka may do so, he may do many things on that night; but it is a practical way for parents to prevent children from eating damaged and decayed fruits, for there is always a wisdom to be found somewhere in folk tales passed through generations.

The Pooka is not much seen in that area nowadays. Perhaps he was chased out when the reservoir was formed in the 1930s or perhaps he hopped away in the previous century when a 7km extension to the Dublin and Blessington steam tramway was built by the Blessington and Poulaphouca Steam Tramway, with its end-of-line terminus at Poulaphouca. It opened for business on 1 May 1895, with great hope and determination. However, the line closed down again in 1932, not long before the great flooding came to this part of Wicklow.

The locality was more memorable for a long time in the world of hunting as being the scene of the destruction of the Kildare hounds in 1813. A description of what happened appeared a good many years later in the *Sporting Magazine* for 1832, after which time the story had matured almost to the status of legend.

The hounds met in November 1813, it was said, at Tipper crossroads, near Naas in neighbouring Co. Kildare. They first sought quarry in neighbouring gorse but raised nothing there and so were trotting towards Troopersfields in the general direction of Blessington and its environs. A large fox – what else? – sprung up from a thicket immediately in front of the hounds and made straight for the Wicklow Mountains, over so rough a country and at such a pace that the whole field was thrown into momentary confusion, with the exception of two foxhunters who, being well mounted, were able to keep the fleeing fox well in sight.

According to the tale, the fox ascended into the hills, soon passing through the soft sedges at Liffey Head, where the river first rises that flows down over Poulaphouca waterfall with such force. Without pausing much for breath, the fox found himself and his followers many miles away in the Vale of Avoca. The distance allegedly travelled was 19km, nearly all against the rising hill over a high and rugged ridge of rocks and streams, at that time unusually swollen by a succession of rainy weather. This feat was achieved in fifty-five minutes, it was said by the original reporter of the story: a tall tale in itself.

On the fox's return to Poulaphouca, it made for a narrow part of the gorge above the waterfall where the river passed between two large rocks. He attempted to jump from one to the other to escape his tormentors but, despite his determination, the tired fox lost his footing and was precipitated into the torrent below.

The waterfall was measured in three sections rushing through a 12m wide chasm lined on either side with Greywacke rock. The entire force of the River Liffey here rushed down to a flat worn basin, which caused the waters to form a rotary eddying motion on impact.

It was bad enough for the huntsmen to see their quarry killed by other means than theirs, as they believed, but imagine their shock when twenty-five hounds who were leading the chase at the time, with equally desperate determination, jumped straight down after the fox and in turn were carried away by the flood, to perish in the swollen waters below the huntsmens' horrified eyes. All except one, that is.

When Grennan, one of the huntsmen, reached the bank of the river, the fox and hounds were all in one struggling melee in the foaming eddies under the thundering fall, some killed in the descent, others maimed but still alive. Only one later succeeded in making the bank, though in an exhausted condition.

Grennan stood for some time like a statue, unable to reach his beloved hounds or assist them in any way. It is said that when he was assured – by their lifeless remains floating in the pool below the waterfall – of the loss of two particular favoured veterans, the master of hounds could stand it no longer. He burst into tears and wept long and bitterly.

The resilient fox managed to reach the bank, though whether he escaped with his life at that time is not recorded, but some contemporary reviewers of this tale maintain that the fox survived and ran with baying followers from near Naas in Co. Kildare to the height of Sally Gap in Wicklow and back to Poulaphouca. Liffey Head near Kippure Mountain is about 457m high, and not less than 24km from the meeting place, over as rough a piece of country as could be found in wild Wicklow. The run thither, and return to almost the starting point – about 50km – was all done in fifty-five minutes.

Another hunt took place, much earlier, in 1744, on the far side of the county, where it borders south Dublin county along the coastline. As the first story wandered across the boundaries of Wicklow and Kildare to the west, this one wanders between Dublin and Wicklow in the east, showing that a fox cares little for man's confines.

It is commemorated in a poem written by a Fr Fleming, a diocesan priest who was formerly a commissioned officer in the Austrian service, such were the career paths of the day.

KILRUDDERY HUNT

Hark, hark, jolly sportsmen, a while to my tale,
Which to pay your attention I'm sure cannot fail;
'Tis of lads, and of horses, and dogs that ne'er tire,
Over stone walls and hedges, through dale, bog and briar;

A pack of such hounds, and a set of such men,
'Tis a shrewd chance if ever you meet with again:
Had Nimrod, the mightiest of hunters, been there,
'Fore God, he had shook like an aspen for fear.

In seventeen hundred and forty and four,
The fifth of December, I think 'twas no more,
At five in the morning by most of the clocks,
We rode from Kilruddery in search of a fox.

The Laughlinstown landlord, the bold Owen Bray,
And Squire Adair, sure, was with us that day,
Joe Debill, Hall Preston, that huntsman so stout,
Dick Holmes, a few others, and so we set out.

We cast off our hounds for an hour or more,
When Wanton set up a most terrible roar;
'Hark to Wanton!' cried Joe, and the rest were not slack,
For Wanton's no trifler esteem'd in the pack.

Old Bonny and Collier came readily in,
And every hound join'd in the musical din;
Had Diana been there she'd been pleas'd to the life,
And one of the lads got a goddess to wife.

Ten minutes past ten was the time of the day
When Reynard broke cover, and this was the way;
As strong from Killegar as though he could fear none,
Away he brushed round by the house of Kilternan.

To Carrickmines thence, and to Cherriwood, then
Steep Shankhill he climbed, and to Ballyman glen.
Bray common he crossed, leap'd Lord Anglesea's wall,
And seem'd to say, 'Little I value you all.'

He ran Bush's grove, up to Carbury Byrn's;
Joe Debill, Hall Preston, kept leaping by turns;
The earth it was open, yet he was so stout,
Though he might have got in, he chose to keep out.

To Malpas' high hill was the way then he flew –
At Dalkey-stone common we had him in view;
He drave on by Bullock, through shrub Glanagery,
And so on to Monk'stown, where Laury grew weary.

Through Rochestown wood like an arrow he pass'd,
And came to the steep hills of Dalkey at last;
There gallantly plung'd himself into the sea,
And said in his heart, 'Sure none dare follow me.'

But soon, to his cost, he perceiv'd that no bounds
Could stop the pursuit of the staunch-mettled hounds;
His policy here did not serve him a rush,
Five couple of Tartars were hard at his brush.

To recover the shore, then, again was his drift,
But ere he could reach to the top of the cliff,
He found both of speed and of running a lack,
Being waylaid and killed by the rest of the pack.

At his death there were present the lads that I've sung,
Save Laury, who, riding a garron, was flung:–
Thus ended, at length, a most delicate chase,
That held us five hours and ten minutes.

We return'd to Kilruddery's plentiful board,
Where dwell hospitality, truth, and my lord;
We talk'd o'er the chase, and we toasted the health
Of the men that ne'er struggled for places of wealth.

'Owen Bray baulk'd a leap', says Hall Preston, ''twas odd';
''Twas shameful', cried Jack, 'by the great living G—d!'
Said Preston, 'I halloo'd, "Get on though you fall,
Or I'll leap over you, your blind gelding and all".'

Each glass was adapted to freedom and sport,
For party affairs we consign'd to the court;
Thus we finish'd the rest of the day and the night
In gay flowing bumpers and toasts of delight.

Then, till the next meeting, bid farewell each brother,
So some they went one way, and some went another;
And as Phoebus befriended our earlier roam,
So Luna took care in conducting us home.

And so they dispersed, but who knows what ghostly foxes watched
them wend their way homewards, still alive, for now.

18

OF WATER
AND STONE

If the Wicklow hills are inhabited by ghosts at all then many of them must surely reside around Ballyknockan village on the hill above what is now the Poulaphouca reservoir, or Blessington Lakes. Many more must inhabit the drowned farmhouses beneath the man-made lake. The lake was formed by damming a floodplain where the King's river joined the Liffey, displacing a traditional community on the lake's inception in 1939, when some 6,500 acres were flooded with river water to provide a water supply and hydroelectricity for Dublin city. According to the plan, some 20 million gallons of water a day would be made available to the capital city, while the dam would generate 30 million units of electricity.

Protests were made, in vain, by people living in the most affected villages of Lacken and Valleymount. An association was set up to fight the compulsory acquisition of land, but the national interest was quoted and protests were drowned. The people of the area then faced long journeys by high roads around the waters to interact with friends and families. Some of them, whose entire holdings were inexorably swamped with water, moved away to Kildare or Dublin and left their memories behind them, deep below the lake waters.

In the emptied houses, thatch was burned off, bridges were demolished. New concrete bridges were built above the intended high-water line; healthy buildings that were to be submerged were demolished; salvage materials were sold off, in many cases to the former owners; and trees and bushes were cut down.

Lacken Holy Well, which was said to have healing powers and had a procession made to it on Mayday, was relocated and the original well submerged.

Some families could trace their lineage back through 600 years in the area. When it was realised that the reservoir would cover a graveyard at Burgage, a decision was made to rebury the remains of the valley's deceased in a new cemetery on higher ground north of Blessington. Local lore says that a 500-year-old cross in the cemetery shed blood, after it was moved to the new location. The original graveyard held 854 graves, many containing multiple burials. Most of the burials were from the mid-1800s, when the famine struck, but burials continued until 1939, when the grave-yard was closed for moving, and one stone dated from the time of the Williamite Wars in 1690.

In 1830, a decade and a half before blight hit the potato crop and heralded the famine, Elizabeth Smith of Edinburgh married Colonel Henry Smith of Baltiboys, Co. Wicklow, who inherited a neglected estate. It had been abandoned during the 1798 rebellion by his late brother, John. The couple set out to restore the house and to restore and develop the farms. A diary that Elizabeth kept reflects the worst days of the famine locally.

In January 1847 she wrote that the frightful reality of it was to be seen in every face. Many had no work and no money; they were cold, naked, hungry and many homeless. By contrast, her own estate of Baltiboys was in comfort, with few of its tenants or staff in real distress.

A cow was killed and a large pot of good soup was made daily at one o'clock, with the soup served to more than twenty people. Firing from the estate was provided for warmth in the homes of its tenants and staff. Elizabeth recorded that beyond the bounda-ries of the estate a dense population squatted here and there upon neglected properties, dying with want. In the wider area, a relief committee resolved to institute soup kitchens for general relief, to be supported by subscription, each subscriber to have a certain number of tickets to distribute. Nonetheless, many died through those years, either from famine or the cholera epidemic that followed in 1849.

One hundred years later, the new reservoir was to lap the townland of Baltiboys and cover what would have been seen as the final resting place of many of the victims, in the cemetery at nearby Burgage.

The original Burgage on the shore of the lake is today dominated by an old crumbling towerhouse, with remains located nearby. Most of the dwellings in the valley were simple single-storey thatched houses with few rooms. Only a better-off family lived in a two-storey home with a slate roof. Landlords reserved slate roofing for farm buildings, not the homes of tenants. Thatched roofs continued to be common in Wicklow until the 1930s, when fashion replaced thatch with galvanised steel roofs. The old roof was, likely as not, retained underneath the new sheets of corrugated steel to provide a layer of insulation, without which the galvanised roof could be cold in winter or overwarm during summer. A galvanised roof can also be very noisy when it rains. Filtered through a thatch it made less noise to bother those living within.

Before the reservoir flooding, the quality of the land in the valley was mixed. Some of it was commonage in which small farmers shared grazing rights. More of it was bog from which locals cut turf to warm their homes through the winter. Otherwise, the village of Ballyknockan was established locally around a series of granite quarries that were established by entrepreneurs in the nineteenth century. These quarries provided much of the cut granite for building projects in Dublin throughout the 1820s, when there was something of a renaissance in Dublin's development. Ballyknockan stone was used in the construction of Heuston railway station, St Audoen's Church on High Street, Dublin, the RDS showground in Ballsbridge and in the National Museum.

The village that naturally grew around these quarries was inhabited by a large number of highly skilled tradesmen, attracted to the area by the employment to be had working in stone. However, it was a closed trade, passed from father to son, and there was little chance of a dispossessed peasant making his way into the trade.

While the craftsmen used their skills in their employer's business, they also worked on their own dwellings to make them uniquely their own. The presence of so many highly skilled stone-cutters resulted in a distinctive type of architecture in the area, beneath their traditional roofs of thatch and the buildings frequently featured bespoke granite chimneys.

The earliest quarries were worked as hillside quarries where the solid granite of Wicklow mountain was overlain by up to 10m of weathered stone. This top layer of stone was dislodged by the stonecutters with crowbars, levers and wooden wedges, leaving the underlying rock undisturbed. By sheer manpower, allowing for the odd block and tackle and levers, workers extracted the stone and hauled it to the horse and dray for onward journey to the site where it would join other blocks to form a new building.

Perhaps phantoms of the stone-cutters of old are still tapping away in the village. They are likely to be aware of an old story concerning fellow artisans in Glendalough, across the Wicklow Gap.

Masons and labourers who were employed in the task of erecting churches there were observed by St Kevin to be gradually losing that health and vigour which they appeared to have possessed at the commencement of their labours. In modern terms, they were tired and spent too soon.

The reason was soon discovered: their hours of labour were regulated by rising with the lark and lying down with the lamb. But, the lark in the valley rose very early on a summer's day; so early, the workers were hard set to keep going until the lamb lay down for the evening, many hours later.

Rather than changing the hours to suit, as might be the worldly thing to do, the saint prayed that the lark might never again be permitted to sing in the valley of Glendalough. According to tradition, this request was granted by the Lord. How the starting time for a working day was then determined is now lost to us. For some reason, St Kevin seemed not to have been bothered with the lying down time of lambs.

Back in Ballyknockan, carters were expected to be loaded and prepared to begin the horse-drawn journey to Dublin sites on the evening before the day of their use: no starting with the lark for them. Transit of the granite stone was by horse and cart. Up to thirty carts left Ballyknockan late each evening to travel together through Blessington and on the road to Dublin as far as the Embankment near Crooksling where, for those with the inclination to sightsee, the flickering lights and chimney smoke of the city of Dublin was spread out below them.

Most would rest, however. The task of guiding and driving draught horses pulling heavy loads over uneven road surfaces was tiring and onerous. They would feed the horses, and rest them before resuming the journey down to the city to reach their destination in the early hours of the morning. Once unloaded, they turned back towards Wicklow to collect a fresh load of granite hewn from the mountain.

John Kelly, 46, of Newtown, Hollywood, told a story of a time when his grandfather was returning from the town of Ballymore Eustace on the carters' route, with another man and two cows. Ballymore was a post and market town and it is likely they were returning from market after buying the pair of cows, or perhaps they were returning with unsold stock on a slow trading day. At the time, fairs were held in Ballymore Eustace on 20 August and 29 October.

To their surprise, on coming up to Carman's Ford they found that their horses would go no further than the two gates that stood at the side of the road. It took the men two hours to coax the horses to move, said John Kelly. Once at home in Hollywood, a few kilometres down the road, the two men had to dry the sweat of terror from the horses before bedding them down for the night.

In another case, a Mr Doyle of Newton stopped at the same place to light his pipe, in peace, on his journey. He was not long stopped when he heard leaves blowing along the road before him. He looked up from his pipe and was amazed to see a beautiful lady dressed in a lovely green frock, with long hair blowing in the air. The very light shoes on her feet made walking softly along the leaves an easy task for her, he recalled afterwards. Who she was is not known, but many people are said to have seen her.

Who knows what spirits lie along the valleys and glens here; who knows who is watching modern man as he passes along. As elsewhere in Wicklow, there are sounds and sights that are to be wondered at and respected, for who knows with certainty who is sleeping and who is watching, or waiting.

19

FÉAR
GORTACH

A great many years ago three men set out across the Wicklow Mountains on their way to purchase some yearling ewes, if suitable opportunity presented itself for them to do so.

One of them was Malachi Horan, a small farmer and no mean storyteller from the Jobstown area of south Dublin on the cusp of Wicklow. He had set off alone and fell in with the other two on the road, as people did in Ireland of long ago, when many journeys were undertaken on foot. In those days, as now, a travelling companion with the gift of storytelling was welcomed, for storytelling is well known to shorten the road.

They crossed the hills by the old foot roads worn down by countless countrymen before them on their way to or from one part of Wicklow or another. The mountain and bog they passed through was uninhabited, and had been since the famine of the nineteenth century had stripped the countryside of the poor people who lived off the land, growing potatoes to stay alive and to pay the rent on their holdings.

The sweeping views changed from hour to hour for the travellers. Summer cloud-shadows swept across the slopes, while rain and storm lurked in the distance, ready to surprise the unwary traveller.

They met multitudes of Irish hares running around, though at a distance from them. The same hares can look enormous in a mist when it swirls about their legs. Their long shadows often give rise

to stories of strange beings flitting through the landscape. Some sit up on their imperious ends against the skyline, like lords of the realm, and stare at people as they are travelling by.

Horan said afterwards that it was very lonesome up in those hills on that day. The hills are so full of old, ancient times that there is something about those places that makes a man glad of company, and gladder still when he has passed them.

It being a fine day, and the three men in fine company, it didn't take them long to reach Sally Gap, Ireland's highest crossroads at almost 500m above sea level. Not being on the tarmac military road that wends its way across the peaks of Wicklow from north to south, including straight through Sally Gap, they could take all the shortcuts that they each knew along the sheep paths through the furze, or any others that were presented to their healthy stride as they rambled along with quip and story and the odd line of a song.

In the high hills there are beliefs brought down through folklore that may appear to the listener in a well-lit rambling house to be nothing other than the imagination of the old people known to have walked the high places, talking to flying hares in the mist. Such listeners may mock, but what is dismissed in warm and convivial company can come back to us in harsh and chilling reality when we are alone, or when we are faced with our own human weakness.

Horan said he was in great heart on that particular day and had never felt better in his life. Then all of a sudden, without leave or notice, he was assailed by a sensation that others have experienced in the high passes. Without a moment's warning, a terrible feeling took hold of him. His stomach was suddenly afflicted by the most awful hunger, his knees shook and the sight left his eyes. That was frightening enough, but a cold sweat broke out on him that nearly froze his blood in his veins.

Other victims of a similar malaise recorded that their innards went from them; that perspiration broke out all over and they were terribly tired all of a sudden, no matter how frisky they had been just a moment before.

In Horan's case, he fell to his hands and knees and thought that he would die within a few minutes.

But for every ailment there is a remedy.

An old antidote to the seizure is to encourage the afflicted one to swallow some oaten bread, as soon as possible. One of the men he had fallen into step with in crossing the hills was a knowledgeable man and was aware of this.

He hastened to the fallen man as quickly as he could and, reaching into his pocket, took out a morsel of bread which he forced into Horan's mouth. Many years later, Horan said that it had been a hard matter for him to swallow what was placed in his jaws by his concerned comrade. But he had managed to hold the bread in his teeth for a while and to swallow it as best he could manage in his frightened and weakened state. And then, in less time than it takes to tell the tale, the life returned into his body. He stood up, tall and erect, and was as well as ever, if deeply disturbed by his sudden encounter with death, unexpected as it had been on that fine day on the height of a Wicklow mountain. The other man told him that he had trodden on *an féar gortach*, 'the hungry grass', without minding where he was going. So it was that Horan was blessed that he had fallen into step with someone who knew what to do in such a circumstance.

The man told Horan that no one but a fool would tramp the hills of Wicklow without food in his pocket when the grass was known to kill even cattle or sheep. Many a stranger died for lack of food in his pocket, he added for good effect.

Whether the man was right or wrong, from that day onwards to the end of Horan's days he never faced that country without bread in his pocket, in case he once more met the hungry grass on his travels.

Horan describes it in appearance as being a white, grass-like herb, a coarse grass that looks like keeb. It lies lank in autumn and mostly grows by the sheep tracks across the high parts of the hills.

To the south of Sally Gap lies a barrier ridge of hills known as the Faragutha Mountains, whose name, taken from *féar gortach*, refers to the widespread belief that the traveller who unknowingly walks upon a certain plant will be suddenly struck down with great faintness and hunger. The best remedy, according to the late J.B. Malone, a twentieth-century expert on hillwalking and mountain lore in Wicklow, is said to be an instant mouthful of homemade currant bread.

His contention was that heavy work and trudging at high altitudes makes drastic demands on the blood's sugar levels, causing sudden and unforeseen weakness. The Faragutha Mountains have the largest area of high ground and heavy going in Wicklow, which Malone asserted confirms the old belief of the consequences of stepping on hungry grass.

Other stories come to us from other storytellers. Some say that the hungry grass goes back to famine times when the sheep tracks formed part of a *slí marbh* as people carried a coffin on their shoulders, from where the person passed away to the graveyard of their choice. The chosen cemetery could have been many parishes distant and all to be walked, every step of the way, in those days of poverty.

However, the coffin bearers were only human and from time to time they would rest the cheap coffin on the ground while they took their ease. Then they would hoist it onto their shoulders once more and be on their way across hill and glen on their sorrowful journey to the final resting place of the departed soul.

It was believed by many that the place where the coffin rested was the place where the hungry grass grew ever afterwards. It was said by those who know that anyone stepping on it experienced the pain of the deceased victim of the famine. Other tradition bearers say that the hungry grass grows where victims of the great hunger of the 1840s fell down for the last time, their mouths stained green with the nettles and grass they had eaten in their starving dementia as they fought unsuccessfully for the life that was leaving their bodies. The spot where the hungry grass grows is where their mouth last touched the ground, so the old story says.

Others have an equally sad and horrifying explanation for the sudden onset of confusion and weakness where *féar gortach* grows.

In the Ireland of long ago, when most of the population was Catholic, the official word of the Church and its priests and bishops ruled the waking conscience of the people. That Church said that the soul of a newborn child who died without being baptised could not be admitted to Heaven and must remain in Limbo. This was interpreted to mean that an unbaptised child could not be buried in the consecrated ground of the parish graveyard.

It was the practice for the father of the dead child to take the tiny body away on his own. He would tell few, if anyone, where he had buried the tiny corpse. Thus it was, people said, that babies were laid to rest in the mountains, where the location was remote and where they would not be disturbed by accident of husbandry.

It is not too far a stretch of belief for some people to say that on such tiny burial places grows the hungry grass to mark where the lost soul lies, awaiting a spiritual resolution of their unfulfilled state.

Whatever the truth of the matter, hungry grass seems to exist on the high passes of Wicklow and whether the condition arises from within a man's own labouring, or from a legacy of the dreadful famine or from a religious belief, it is as well to carry some bread or biscuits on the journey up there, ready to meet what lies on the high hills where silence awaits.

20

Derrybawn Cow

It seems that Fionn Mac Cumhaill left his mark everywhere he went, not least in Wicklow and in Glendalough in particular, long before the better-known St Kevin came along to say his prayers there.

Kevin is said to have arrived in Glendalough in the sixth century and to have founded an early Christian monastery by the dark waters of the mountain lakes. After the saint's death the place attracted not only a large number of ecclesiastics, but also a lay population seeking solace and personal contentment.

Not surprisingly, a town of sorts grew up in the area, with many people moving to work and trade there. The remains of a number of stone churches, an intact round tower and crosses can be seen by the modern visitor.

However, the story of the Derrybawn Cow does not concern saints or prayers, though there is an element about it of matters unknown to man.

Glendalough is a glacial valley formed during the Ice Age which, as everyone knows, was some 20,000 years ago. It is known as the glen of the two loughs, or lakes, which were created when the ice melted away and people began to swim and sunbathe once more. Millions of years before that, a collision of continental plates resulted in the formation of the Wicklow Mountains, but there are few people alive now who remember that day.

On the southern side of Glendalough, Lugduff Mountain towers over the Upper Lake, Mullacor is midway between Glendalough and the next glen, south at Glenmalure. The oak-footed Derrybawn sits quietly above the spot where, in present times, visitors park their cars. And where, in 1835, stood a smelter house and ore-grinding mill associated with an ore extraction and processing site from Glendalough mines.

An old man who was born in nearby Glenmalure said in the late 1990s that he had a number of children and they all went to California, with what he could give them. Once there, they bought a bit of a field. However, when they put in the plough, it stuck fast. Perplexed, they looked underneath it, and there was fine gold stretched within the earth, said the emigrants' father. He said that his children were made rich, and that their daughters were riding on fine horses with new saddles and elegant bits in their mouths. Yet not a ha'porth did they ever send home to their father in the hills. For his own part he wished that the Devil might ride with them to hell. And maybe he did, for a father scorned is an angry father.

But the story told by Máirín Ní Broin, who attended Glendalough school in the years 1934-38, took place long before a car park or visitors' centre was envisaged for the glen.

A break in the strata in the mountain of Derrybawn, which is composed of mica slate, is called the Giants Cut, mainly because one part has sunk many feet below the other. However, local lore states that the defile was caused when Fionn Mac Cumhaill was in an angry mood one day and smote the mountain with his sword, creating the division in the hill that anyone can see to this day.

At the base of Derrybawn Mountain sits a bullaun stone, a granite stone with a single conical basin and curved sides. It is known as the Deer Stone, from an old story that a deer shed its milk in the basin for St Kevin to drink.

Sometimes it is hard to know where fact and folklore blend and the fanciful story takes over from the prosaic everyday.

According to a story recorded midway through the twentieth century by Máirín Ní Broin of Glendalough school, there was once a man who owned a herd of cows and who had seven sons, none of whom had gone out to America to find gold or buy a field there. The family grazed the cows around Derrybawn. As was the custom of the day, the man hired a boy to herd the animals for him on the hills and especially around Doire Bán, Derrybawn. All went well for a time until the man noticed that one particular cow gave more milk than the others. He wondered why this should be and asked the boy if he knew any reason why this cow should be yielding more. But the boy could not give a reason that made any sense to the animal's owner. So he instructed the herd boy to pay particular attention to that animal so that they could reflect on why it was producing more profit than the others after its daily grazing on the hillside of Derrybawn.

Well, the boy was as perplexed as anyone else as to why one animal was producing more milk than the others. He watched for a few days and could see no difference between them. Then he decided on an old herds' boy trick: he would follow the cow's tail all day and leave the others to fend for themselves, for as long as it took.

Next morning, when it came time to lead the animals out onto the grazing area, he stationed himself behind the particular cow and watched to see which way she went. To make doubly sure, he held onto the animal's swishing tail before it started to move.

It ambled along at first and then picked up a shambling pace until it reached a trench, which surrounded a place that had been fortified at some stage in times past. According to the story gathered by Máirín Ní Broin, the mound was called Round Mote. The herd boy watched as the cow leaned in and began to lick at something that the young boy couldn't see.

He pushed the protesting cow away from whatever was taking its interest so much that it would leave the herd to graze alone in the rocks.

There are some things that you are glad you find and there are others you would be just as glad you never had to come across.

The boy peered closer at what was before him. He wanted to be sure of what was there, as he didn't want to appear foolish when reporting back to his employer on this favoured cow's secret.

For there in front of him was a pair of human feet, not the sort of thing a traveller might expect to find on the hill on a day's ramble, much less a terrified herd boy carrying out his employer's instructions.

The feet were bare white flesh, the feet of a person and not of a skeleton. Nicks and cuts visible on the skin showed that the owner of the feet had not favoured the wearing of shoes overmuch in his life, a common enough situation in the Wicklow of the time. People at that time did not begin to wear boots until they were 20 years of age, when their feet were supposed to be grown full-sized.

It is said that people in the olden days did not have bad feet as a result. Any corns or the like that appeared were cured with bog water. Those afflicted with chiropodial problems worked in the bog with bare feet for a few days, as a cure. It was said that James Kearney of Cryhelp, 3 miles east of Dunlavin, did not wear boots

until he was 60 years of age. The people who knew him said he died in hospital of old age.

All this was known to the herd boy; but he had never in his short life heard tell of a pair of feet talking to a living person, which was what was happening now. Or at least that was what he thought; but in reality it was a voice in his head, or in the air, that he heard.

The voice told him to take the rest of the body of which the feet were the only part he could see and to bury it in consecrated ground. He stood stock still in pure shock, as it was clear to him that he lacked the physical prowess to lift a body, carry it elsewhere and bury it, even allowing that the priest, the authorities and his employer would allow him to do such a thing.

So, he drove the cows home once more and told his employer what had happened.

The man retraced the boy's steps to where the feet still lay. Satisfied with his preliminary investigation, the man went to the priest and asked for permission to rebury the lost soul in consecrated ground, to which the priest assented, not quite knowing how the feet and body had come to be buried in the mound in the first place.

The man asked his seven sons to go with the herd to where the body was hidden. They were to dig out the remains and bring them to the space in the graveyard specified by the priest. However, according to the story, one son refused to participate in the sad ritual. He told his father that it had nothing to do with him and he would not go with his brothers and the herd to the Mote. The father instead urged the others to carry out the wishes of the poor soul who had spoken to the herd boy.

Three days in five bring rain across Wicklow's mountains, it is said, but prolonged rainstorms are rare. Nonetheless, the wet slopes of sedges squelched underfoot as the silent men transported and interred the body in consecrated ground, as requested.

The objecting son took his hounds onto Derrybawn as his brothers intoned a silent prayer below in the graveyard. Those who know the tale said that he felt justified in himself that he had followed the correct course. Until, that is, his hounds turned on him and sprang at his unsuspecting body. They were not long about tearing him to pieces, for these were hunting dogs, used to tearing flesh from a living body.

His grieving brothers found but little evidence of his passing when they went in search of him on the mountain of Derrybawn above silent Glendalough.

The cows resumed milking, neither one nor the other exceeding her sisters in production. No matter what fate had befallen the missing son, he never returned to create problems for anyone minding cows on a Wicklow hillside.

21

BEDDING
ST KEVIN

The valley of Glendalough, or the Valley of the Two Lakes in English, was also commonly called the Seven Churches. It is situated in the barony of Ballinacor, 50km from Dublin. The glen is about 4km in extent, having lofty and precipitous mountains hanging over it on every side, except on that by which it is entered between Derrybawn on the south and Broccagh Mountain on the north.

At the time when St Kevin established his religious community there, the eastern extremity of the glen was an extensive meadow of waving grass, watered by a deep and clear stream that was fed by the lakes in the valley, and abounding with excellent brown trout, and water and food aplenty for the community that was to grow up around the ecclesiastical settlement.

A narrow road led into the glen, where daylight is constricted by the precipitous cliffs overhanging the steep sides of the glen and where waterfowl skim along the surface of the lakes. Kevin and his monks, in their day, must have sat and wondered at the profound stillness of it all.

Kevin came to Glendalough in the sixth century, to live the life of an ascetic monk. He lived in solitude for seven years, sleeping on a dolmen perched on a perilous precipice below Lugduff on the southern side of the Upper Lake. It is said that he was led there by an angel. But, if this is so, it was hardly the same angel that led the beautiful Cathleen there after him.

Before that, however, other monks joined him and development of a spiritual community began. Situated about 9m from the brown surface of the lake is what is now known as St Kevin's Bed, a small cave, capable of containing three people at a squeeze, not bigger inside than a baker's small oven. Approach is by a narrow path and then a scramble along the steep side of the overhanging mountain. Every step must be considered and taken carefully, for the slightest false step will tumble the unwary pilgrim into the watery lake below.

Long after Kevin was gone to his heavenly reward for his saintly deeds, the rebel leader Michael Dwyer made use of the cave to conceal himself from searching Crown forces in the years after the failed rebellion of 1798, when redcoats pursued rebels through the hills of Wicklow.

For several days, a body of Highlanders had been in close pursuit of Dwyer, who took shelter at St Kevin's Bed, long since abandoned by men of religion and their camp followers. Exhausted, and having fallen fitfully asleep, Dwyer was nearly taken when the Highlanders came upon him by stealth; however, the startled sleeper, ever a precarious man to capture, had time to leap from the cave into the lake below. He struck out slowly for the far shore, dressed as he was in heavy clothing for his travels on the hills.

The frustrated Highlanders found it impossible to carry their long muskets with them at speed along the difficult pathway they had lately traversed with such caution and determination. Despite their efforts they could not make sufficient haste to circumnavigate the lake to meet the swimming rebel once he reached land. Dwyer made the opposite shore without molestation, and went on to vanish into the hills once more.

But that was long after another body had entered the lake at the very same spot, that time aided by St Kevin himself. Kevin came from a wealthy family, though no records exist of his time before he entered the religious life. He embraced the life of a holy man and was to lend his name to a period of industrious activity for religiously minded individuals.

Nonetheless, folklore links his name with the fair Cathleen who was descended of an illustrious race and who wanted for no material thing in her life. Having heard of the fame of the young St Kevin, she went to listen to his religious vision when he preached.

But she was young and he was possessed of an aura of other worldly saintliness, so some unholy thoughts crept in amidst the telling of her rosary and other prayers. In short, she became enamoured of the youthful saint, though more for his manly ways than for his preaching on matters spiritual. Her infatuation with him caused him not to build his abbey at Luggelaw, on the margin of Lough Tay some miles away in the high hills, as the repeated visits of Cathleen, while Kevin lived there, persuaded him to remove to some retreat where he might be free of her interest. Instead he ultimately decided upon Glendalough.

But a determined admirer is hard to lose. Just when he had established his seminary, and supposed himself at rest for the remainder of his mortal time, the beauteous but unhappy Cathleen renewed her visits to him. He was somewhat dismayed at this turn of events, as would be any aspiring saint whose thoughts were on the next world and his place therein.

The lovely and passionately enamoured young Cathleen begged to be permitted to live in sight of him, to look upon his shadow, to hear not even his voice but its echo. In exchange, she said she would lie like a canine companion at his feet, take penance for his sins, as well as her own, and forget her own soul for the good of his, in prayer.

Determined to avoid the temptations of so much innocence, cupidity and fidelity in one so fair, and to spare her tender feelings, the saint withdrew to his remote stony bed in the inaccessible cave below Lugduff and above the calm lake water.

Nevertheless, once embarked on her journey of worship, and determined to press her case for affection, day after day Cathleen visited the known haunts of her beloved Kevin, but he was nowhere to be found. It was small wonder, for he was inside the cave saying his prayers in the hope that she would not find him and, growing weary, would leave him alone.

Nonetheless, even a saint cannot think of everything. Kevin had a favourite dog that knew a good deal more about his habits than Kevin ever realised. It happened that one morning, as the disconsolate Cathleen was moving slowly along the churchyard path, seeking Kevin or his presence, this favourite dog met and fawned upon her and, like a traitor, turned swiftly and led her to his master's hidden home.

Once there, Cathleen saw her beloved was asleep.

In a reversal of most folktales, in which the maiden awaits the kiss of her suitor to arise and live happily ever afterwards, there then followed, however, a most uncharitable part of the future saint's conduct. On awaking in his hiding place and perceiving a female leaning over him, he was quite perturbed. Neither man nor woman should be there with him, and certainly not this woman over whom he had decamped from one part of Wicklow to another.

Since Kevin was a mortal man, given to the weaknesses of the flesh, he rose up in righteous arousal to address his ever-ardent follower. He would, of course, have pointed out to her that there was little chance of him abandoning the path to sainthood, there in Glendalough, to go and live with her people somewhere else. But Cathleen was nothing if not determined. Having come this far, she would have insisted that love would find a way, though probably without being too specific on how this was to transpire, for fear of frightening off the other-worldly Kevin and losing him forever.

Words failing him, Kevin fell to praying for what he desired, which truth to tell was to see the back of his tormentor forever.

Some say that his prayer was only half answered, though it is hard to say whether this was due to a certain reticence on his part to fully commit to the intent of his exhortation, or whether the Heavens above drew the line at drowning one soul at the behest of another.

Whether or not his wish was only half granted, Cathleen drifted up from the ground that she stood upon and floated out, somewhat surprised, over the water of the lake. She faded into a light mist and dissipated, never to be seen again, while Kevin who had spurned her well-meaning mortal advances went on to become a well-known saint.

Others say that Cathleen was drowned, there and then, and that it served her right for attempting to interfere with a holy man intent on saying his prayers. Though that is to impose an outsider's

view on the matter, when neither party can now attest to what happened between two people in the seclusion of the small cave above the waters of the Upper Lake.

Indeed, who is to say that Cathleen did not in fact stumble and fall into the lake water below? What, then, would she have done if she hadn't drowned instantly, other than to swim to safety on the far sloping shore where Dwyer so many years later clambered to safety?

One version of the story says that this is exactly what happened. For a brief while on the northern margin of the lake, Cathleen was seen wringing out her flowing locks to be rid of the waters of Glendalough from her hair and clothes, forever.

In any case, whatever way she left the presence of the good man, Cathleen took her leave of him, either as a wraith, a drowned body, or a soaked and spurned suitor. She was never seen in the area again, not as ghost, follower or avenging angel. Small wonder, for there is only so much a person can do to press their suit to another whose mind is set firmly on some other world.

22

DARGLE
LOVERS

The Dargle Valley in Co. Wicklow is said to be haunted by the spirit of a young girl who fell to her untimely death on the eve of St John's Day when her romance ended in mistaken tragedy.

She appears in a different form on a given night not far to the south of the old village of Enniskerry. Legend has it that the ghost of the sorrowing girl flits along in the shape of a white fawn, forever seeking her wronged lover in the surrounding woodlands.

It was the custom throughout the country for bonfires to be built at sunset on the eve of St John's Day. The fire had to be tended till long after midnight. Prayers were said, to obtain God's blessing on the crops, which were then at the peak point of summer bloom.

Jumping through the flames was thought by young people to bring health and long life. It was said that the act protected the jumpers from accidents, ailments, epidemics and the effects of witchcraft or the evil eye. There were some who claimed they could tell by the demeanour of a jumper whether they had been false, or true, to their beloved.

The Dargle river rises high up in the hills between War Hill and Tonduff, then tumbles along before passing through a winding narrow gorge. About midway down the glen stands a huge mass of rock, projecting at a great height over the river. From this point, a lover's eye can see every part of the glen below, where at intervals the river breaks over fragments of rock that have detached from the cliffs above and remain where they have fallen.

Lover's Leap rock rises above the old trees, offering views over a broad canopy of mixed woodlands to the summits of hills beyond. The river below rushes over a series of rapids, providing a deceptively soothing background to a romantic tryst. In mid-summer, the air is full of birdsong and all is well with the world.

Two storytellers recorded what happened here; yet though they differ slightly in their telling, the difference in storytelling merely makes the essential story ring truer, for no two storytellers ever tell the one story in the same way.

Patrick Kennedy said that Mary, a capricious damsel of the neighbourhood, showed some particular interest in one of her lovers, whose name was Edward, while she was secretly attracted to another man of the area. A besotted Edward displayed too much devotion to her, and paid too much attention to her slightest wishes, for he found himself being asked to go hither, thither and yon to fetch and carry for her for the slightest reason.

On one fateful day, she expressed a desire for a certain kind of necklace that could only be had from the city of Dublin, some miles away. Naturally, Edward said he would at once start out to Dublin to get it. Mary told him not to tire himself with a double journey there and back; he should not think of returning that day.

She saw him off with great solicitude and anticipated gratitude for the necklace she coveted so much. Her thankfulness proved to be her downfall, for the lovelorn Edward was so anxious to gratify his lady love with the ornament for her fair throat, and to display his own zeal, that he did not allow himself such indulgence as staying overnight in Dublin. As he left for the city he knew that he would return that same evening, all the better to surprise his true love. Days were at their longest and he would return while it was still bright.

So it was that late on the same evening a returned Edward was hurriedly walking along the bank high over the Dargle towards Mary's house, when on a mossy hillock nearby he discovered her, listening with every sign of loving interest to the discourse of the secretly favoured rival.

Her suggestion that Edward stay overnight in Dublin was exposed now as an artifice to keep him away so she could enjoy the attentions of his rival in love, and still welcome Edward's return on the following day with her prize.

Edward drew out the necklace from the safekeeping of his grey coat pocket, where he had made sure many times on the journey that it was safe. He approached the spot where Mary and the other man lay on the lush green grass of summer, the other man oblivious to Edward's approach. A startled Mary, sensing and then seeing his distraught approach, could only watch as Edward laid the shiny necklace on the grass before her, his false love.

She watched him with growing dread as he walked to the edge of the nearby overhanging rock, and plunge down, smashing through bushes and shrubs in his deathly descent to an abrupt stop below. At that moment, even the birdsong seemed stilled.

Others heard the commotion and flocked about in efforts to recover his body from the swirling brown mountain water. They managed to reach him, but his spirit had departed. His broken form was recovered and carried to church and then to the grave-yard to be buried.

Mary deeply mourned the loss of her lover, for she had never intended her actions to have such repercussions.

In the time that followed, she was told many times that time would heal the wound and that memory would fade. But, no matter how the girl employed herself in the long days and weeks after the tragedy of her betrayal, the dismal clang of the funeral bell for her dead lover never left her ears.

Mary spent her days recalling the happy times with Edward when all had seemed possible. And from constant dwelling on his tragic fate she became distraught with grief, slowly but inexorably.

She took to haunting the fatal spot where she had been discovered and where her mortal eyes had last seen the living Edward before his tumble from the high rock.

The insane are said to see more than the sane ever do, and who is to deny what happened next, or say it is untrue?

For Mary came to see the ghost of Edward on the hillock by the rock above the waters below. No others could see him, but Mary insisted she could.

It was not long before she began to believe that Edward was calling to her. She said her lover beckoned to her to come to him from the opposite side of the ravine.

Eventually, distraught with grief and elated at her imminent reunion with Edward, Mary leapt from the identical spot as he had done on the steep jagged outcrop of rock above the glen. She perished, in her turn, as her mortal body fell broken onto the stones below.

According to Patrick Kennedy, her spirit is still seen there on the eve of St John's Day, traversing the fatal locality in the form of a milk-white fawn. But the spirit of Edward is not seen, according to the story, so perhaps they have not yet been reconciled.

A more modern writer, the late John J. Dunne, said that Mary had heard a church bell pealing the death of her lover on Midsummer's Eve, a night that now brings their phantom reunion. Every Midsummer's Eve, her ghost is said to appear in the Wicklow glen, eternally seeking the young lover she betrayed.

According to Dunne's tale, Mary was faithless to Edward, giving her attentions instead to another young man who had come to woo her, with dash and charm. However, when she was singing a favourite song to please the new man, she heard the distant toll of a church bell, unmistakably signifying a death and burial, as she paused between verses.

The young expect death the least, and on inquiring for whom the bell tolled, the young woman was horrified to discover that Edward, stricken by her unfaithfulness, had died of a broken heart.

Overcome by remorse, she left her new admirer to his own devices. She hurried to the graveyard where they had just buried the youth who had died of unrequited love for her.

Having missed his sorrowful interment, Mary spent that first night at his freshly covered graveside, weeping and softly calling his name through the Wicklow mountain rain. She returned on each succeeding night and continued a lonely vigil until daylight returned each morning.

Her mind collapsed with the strain and guilt of all that had happened. She confided to her distressed family that Edward, her lover, had risen from the grave and walked with her through Dargle glen, promising to meet her once more at his graveside and to take her to a place where they would be together, forever.

This announcement was met with shock and horror by Mary's family, who moved immediately to confine her to her home; but a lover's determination will surmount all challenge. Mary managed to escape her detention. Although followed at speed by her terrified brother, her swift path took her to the river and its high rock above, before anyone could come upon her.

Mary was seen to climb up the huge crag above the Dargle river, where she paused for a moment before plunging into the laughing tumbling river below.

Perhaps she was lured to her death by the phantom of her rejected lover. Perhaps her belief was confused by her tortured imagination. Nonetheless, whatever she saw was real enough for an otherwise healthy woman to pitch herself onto the unyielding rocks below to end her own mortal life forever.

According to Dunne: each year on the anniversary of that night the spirit of the unhappy girl revisits the height above the river in the shape of a white fawn, dashing forwards and backwards and disappearing into the shadows of the woods, eternally seeking forgiveness of a wronged lover.

While one teller says it is St John's Eve and the other Midsummer's Eve, the stories are essentially the same.

Perhaps the spirits of the Wicklow lovers were united in the waters of the Dargle river as it made its way to the Irish Sea. Or perhaps Edward never called to Mary across that chasm. Perhaps her guilt and her grief drove her into eternity on a warm summer's night in Co. Wicklow, from the rock they now call Lover's Leap.

For love is a strange and a wonderful thing. Spirits of love foregone flit through the soft darkness of a Wicklow night, endlessly twisting and turning in the eternal search for true contentment.

23

THE DEVIL IS
IN THE GLEN

The stories of the cupidity of two unrelated men circle about Devil's Glen in a curious way; one ends with the escape of an apple thief, the other leaves a scar in the heart of the land, where a mighty tussle took place so very long ago.

The Vartry river rises at the eastern base of Douce Mountain, and nowadays, after flowing some 8km, is caught by a man-made embankment at Roundwood, to form a reservoir that supplies Dublin city with water. The flowing water that escapes from the reservoir tumbles down the narrow and winding ravine of the Devil's Glen.

Geologists say the glen was gradually cut out by meltwater during the glacial period as the river entered at the waterfall to fall to a rocky bed below. Before the Vartry Reservoir was built higher up, the river came through the glen in full force. The roaring of the water in flood was so loud at times that locals said the Evil One was howling for sinners in the ravine. For it was said that the opening of the gorge was cut out of the hills by the cloven hoof of the Devil himself.

How this came to happen is suggested by a story recalled by Patrick Kennedy in his *Legendary Fictions of the Irish Celts*.

Long ago, he said, the glen was a long low hill, with trees scattered over its surface. In its neighbourhood was a convent, whose novices would enjoy the air under the shades of the trees.

To the great disappointment of many young princes and chiefs, Aoife, the lovely daughter of a neighbouring chieftain, entered the convent as a postulant and, by so doing, placed herself out of bounds to suitors.

However, the convent did not impose strict rules, so it was not difficult to gain sight of the princess and to speak to her. Nonetheless, without exception, every suitor left with a polite though determined refusal.

One such was a young prince who joined in the chorus of praise of the unattainable Aoife. His disappointment was difficult enough to endure, but was made even worse when he was mocked by a sallow-skinned man standing among the other suitors.

The stranger said there was no woman in Ireland who would not be won by either manly beauty or by riches. The young prince disagreed.

The sallow-skinned man continued to assert his beliefs and the young prince continued to disagree with him. The man challenged him to be at the entrance of the convent on the morrow, at noon, when Aoife would be subjected to the influence of beauty, adding that if that failed, then gold would be tried on the following day.

The prince duly turned up and awaited developments. In the distance he heard horns playing an enchanting melody. He saw a mounted chieftain approaching. Light sparkled from his jewel-covered costume at every movement of his magnificent steed. The rider's face and form were those of a beautiful well-formed youth. His retinue all about him were dressed in the most costly of clothing.

The prince, realising what was happening, tried to shout treachery, but an attendant of the sallow-skinned one touched him with a stick, which to the prince's astonishment left him powerless to move or speak.

There he remained until the glittering youth returned from his mission, without success.

Beauty had failed, said the sallow-skinned man, but gold would exert its power on the next day. The prince could not respond. However, once the cohorts had departed, he recovered his faculties.

In dejection, he wandered away to a high point on the hill where an old stone cross stood close to a spring of water. The ground was marshy and the course of the little brook was scarcely to be discerned among the whispering grasses. In weary disappointment, the prince sat down and, suddenly tired, fell asleep.

In his slumber, a beautiful form clothed in white flowing robes, with long hair, appeared to him to tell him she was the Sighe, or fairy, to whom the care of the stream was entrusted. She wished, she said, that the waters should dance and sparkle in the sunshine, and the sounds of its ripples and falls should come to the ears of all men and women.

She told the prince that he could accomplish this for her and, at the same time, punish the demon who sought to turn Aoife away from her beliefs.

When the prince awoke he was not sure whether the dream had been a stirring of his imagination or a message given to him of a task to fulfil.

Still unsure, the following day, he watched as the richly clad youth came along, this time with slaves and horses laden with gold and precious stones. He entered the convent with great presence. The young prince slipped in after him to see what he might see. However, the gold, diamonds and pearls had no more effect on Aoife than had the manly beauty of the wooer. Sensing failure, the suitor begged and prayed in vain, all the while with the young prince remaining hidden behind him. To the young prince's astonishment, he saw a demon's tail escape from under the suitor's fine clothes and begin to lash about in fury.

Before any harm could come to Aoife, the prince flung a pair of praying beads around the thrashing tail. The demon, thwarted by a power greater than his, sprung out of the convent and onto the green hillside beyond. In his fury, he began to over-heat and sped to the spring to cool down; but the shade of the stone cross was on it, now the day had advanced, and the demon dared not approach.

The assembled suitors watched the demon fling himself down, as, overcome by the power of the sacred talisman, he rolled about in agony, tearing away soil and stones alike, and flinging them from him in every direction.

He continued to tear and fling out earth and rocks for the entire length of what became a new glen. Water began to flow down this new avenue. The ground welcomed the coursing of the stream that soon increased to the strength of a goodly mountain river, leaping from ledge to pool.

The demon turned on the young prince, intending to tear him to pieces, but a glance at the beads sent him leaping through the air once more. He departed, swifter than a stone hurled from a strong man's sling.

Now unchallenged, the prince returned to woo Aoife, but he too was unsuccessful. And, if he did not persuade her to be his bride, she instead induced him to become a monk in a neighbouring monastery. Who knows, he may have thought she would change her mind if he stayed around long enough; but if she did, there were no storytellers around to record what happened on that day.

We can only imagine that the nun and the monk, and the Sighe on the hill beside the well, lived tolerably well together forever afterwards.

Many centuries later, when forests had multiplied in Devil's Glen, the glen became the hiding place of scattered unsuccessful insurgents. In order to get rid of them, the powers-that-be decided to set fire to the timber to flush them out. Blackened stumps, like a demon's rotten teeth, long bore witness to the extent of the conflagration.

A long time after that, the family of the playwright John Millington Synge owned land in the area, where he spent some time as a young lad. He recalled that a stone's throw from an old house where he spent several summers was a garden that had been returning to nature for the best part of twenty years. This garden was surrounded by a wall more than 2m high in parts; the grounds were marked by paths beaten out by the feet of numerous small boys who came to steal whatever fruit was available. As with much of the glens of Wicklow, crops were always late in this garden.

In one particular year, the apple crop was unusually plentiful. In recognition of this, thieving raids were made upon it every Sunday by persons unknown. Synge recorded that one particular Sunday he decided to lie in wait for the thieves. He thought the most likely time for the raid would be about noon, when local gaggles of boys made their way home from Mass, and when the Protestant owners of the lands were more than likely attending to their own church services some 5km away, far enough removed to see or hear nothing of the uninvited visitors.

A little before 11 a.m. therefore, Synge slipped out of the house with a book for company, locking the door behind him. Putting the big old key in his pocket, he lay down underneath a bush to await the raiders.

He had forgotten the purpose of his post when he happened to look away from the page and saw a young man, in his best Sunday clothes, walking nonchalantly up the path towards him. The visitor stopped when he saw that he was observed. Not quite knowing what to do next, Synge began to discuss the fineness of the day with the stranger.

However, the pleasantries did not last long before the young lad ran away. In this, he emulated a mountain deer: stock still one moment with watching eye and away with a bound the next.

Synge leapt to his feet and ran after him, seeing for the first time a flock of small boys swarming up the walls of the garden on their way out to the wilds of Wicklow and safety beyond the stockade, now that a chase had begun.

Knowing that the gate was locked, and that if he tried to get over the wall his pursuer would catch him, and that there was no other way out, the youngster ran round and round through the raspberry canes, over the strawberry beds, and in and out among the apple trees.

Though we could safely assume that both Synge and the young lad were in their health, it was heavy going after a time, and both began to tire. Synge caught his foot in a trailing briar on the path and tumbled over, whereupon his quarry rushed to the wall and began scrambling up as fast as his grasping fingers and slipping toes would allow. However, just as he was drawing his trailing leg over the top, a reinvigorated Synge caught him by the heel from below.

Naturally enough, the young lad struggled and kicked back with the trapped foot, and might have succeeded but for the law of physics that saw him brought down by the sheer weight of the hanging body of his pursuer below. The would-be thief landed at the feet of John Millington Synge, an armful of useless masonry along with him.

Synge caught him by the neck to detain him and tried to ask his name, but found they were both too breathless to speak – the one to enquire, the other to respond. They remained there glaring one to another, and gasping painfully for some time, trying to recover. Synge was the first to fill his lungs and, in a whisper, began to upbraid the other for climbing over a person's wall to steal his apples, when to all appearances he was such a fine, well-dressed, young man.

Synge could see that his captive was in dread that he might have him up in the police courts; but Synge had no intention of doing so. Instead, he asked the lad for his name and address. Attempting to win the day, the young lad said he lived about 10km away, and had come there for Mass and to see a friend. Then, the lad said, a thirst had come upon him on the way back, and he thought a juicy apple would slake it for his walk home.

Furthermore, he swore that he would never come over the wall again, if his captor would let him off. Indeed, what's more, he would pray to God to have mercy on him when his last hour would come.

Synge was sure that the story was a lie, so he said there was a woman belonging to the area who was at that moment inside the house helping the girl to cook the Sunday dinner. He invited the silver-tongued lad to walk in with him to see if he was such a stranger as he'd have Synge believe.

Suiting actions to words, Synge took him by the neck and wrist and set off for the gate. However, when they had gone but a pace or two the young lad stopped and said that his cap had fallen on the other side of the wall. He asked permission to cross over and get it.

Synge had had enough of the adventure by then and told him to be off; but if he ever caught him again in the orchard then woe betide him.

He was not entirely surprised a few days later to discover that the intruder lived not a full kilometre away, and was related to a small boy who came to the house every morning to run messages and to clean boots.

It seemed the Devil's Glen had not lost its attraction for those willing to deceive to achieve their end.

24

BRAY
SMUGGLERS

Reports of ghosts flitting about an ancient church on Bray Head in darkness in the 1800s may have been propagated by smugglers to keep prying eyes away. For inside the church, from time to time, were concealed stores of French silks, wine and brandy, lately landed illegally on Bray Head. The ruins of the church of Raheenaclig sit on the hill with a fine view out to sea, all the better to see approaching craft. A literal translation of the Irish name, Raheenaclig, is little rath of the stones, or the little rath of the bell.

Down below, and somewhere on the ground later occupied by Claddagh Terrace, there stood a mud hovel, so tiny, so wretched and so miserable as to earn for it the lofty title of The Rat Hole. This dwelling was tenanted by an eccentric, solitary, tar-begrimed old fisherman. The man took a delight in surrounding his rat hole with ill-smelling heaps of manure, offal, seaweed and every other repugnant thing that came within his reach.

After a while, it became difficult to distinguish between the dwelling and this strange accumulation of noxious scents and aromas. Why he gathered these malodorous accumulations none could construe; but that he enjoyed the possession of them could be open to no doubt, as he was to be seen there during the leisure hours, regaling his nose and eyes on their heady perfume. That is, according to the tale told by Weston St John Joyce, writing 100 years ago in his guide *The Neighbourhood of Dublin*.

Perhaps the fisherman was also a smuggler, hiding his stock from prying nostrils beneath a pile of pongs before he moved them on to another link in the chain of smugglers.

In another cabin on Bray Head itself lived an elderly woman and her daughter, whose public means of livelihood were seeking and selling pebbles, known as Wicklow pebbles. Those pebbles in favour at the time were described as white and almost pellucid, which did not strike fire so well, being imperfect crystals. Variously coloured pebbles are also found all along the Wicklow coast, which do strike fire with steel. These stones could be cut, and responded well to a high polish. However, the two local women were really engaged in the profitable business of smuggling and, along with others, acted as agents for the various overseas craft that then frequented this coast for such trade.

The rocky promontory of Bray Head rises straight from the sea to a height of some 242m. Its spectacular cliffs are home to the gannet, kittiwake, the great black-backed gull and the fulmar. On the lower rocks guillemots, black guillemots, razorbills, shags and cormorants can be seen drying their wings or contemplating lunch. Those folk who went in the summer to enjoy the sea breezes and gaze at swimming seals and passing dolphin amid the raucous cry of the bird population had to pick their way as best they could among the slippery pebbles and sand heaps that then lay along the shore.

The wild and lonely coast of Wicklow offered many facilities for smuggling. Bray Head was particularly suited to the trade, despite the presence of coastguards at Bray and Greystones on either extremity of the Head.

The best efforts of the authorities were unable to accomplish much more than interrupting and delaying the smugglers, for lawbreakers often carried a combination of legitimate and illegal cargo on their vessels. Under cover of night, or misty weather with sea fog rolling in to the waiting land, they off-loaded the contraband into small boats to be carried ashore by native smugglers using personal knowledge of the sea and rocks off Bray Head. Meanwhile, the mother ship sailed on openly with legitimate cargo to nearby Dublin or another port, in all outward innocence. That Revenue and Customs officers in that period could look in the wrong direction undoubtedly helped trade to flourish.

However, matters could become nasty. The *Dublin Weekly Journal* of 26 April 1735 reported that a serious affray between a party of smugglers and local Revenue officers occurred at Bullock, a little way along the coast from Bray: 'Last week, some of the King's officers made a seizure of a large quantity of tea and brandy at Bullock; and next morning several persons attempted to rescue it from the officers, which occasioned a great battle, in which several were wounded on both sides; one Mr. Brown, an officer, was shot through the thigh, and 'tis thought two of the smugglers were killed', said the periodical.

Little wonder, then, that the pebble-gathering mother went about armed and was, at least on one occasion, engaged in an affray with the preventive men, though it seems no one lost their lives as a result. She was known as a woman of great courage and strength of character and had amassed a considerable fortune by her operations. When she died many years afterwards, her daughter was a rich woman.

The principal place of concealment on Bray Head was known as 'The Brandy Hole', which was not in sight of either Bray or Greystones coastguards. In the 1840s, the building of the railway line that ran through it scuppered operations in The Brandy Hole. But, before that, there was an immense cavern there at sea level. Its entrance opened to the sea, and its many caves extended far in under the hill, affording ample accommodation for the cargoes of vessels plying their illegal trade. Into this great natural storehouse, fully laden boats were easily able to make their way by the light of lanterns, and discharge their contents high and dry into the numerous barrels prepared for their arrival.

Immediately over this cavern, and adjoining the rude goat track that then encircled Bray Head, was a shaft sunk in a slanting direction into the earth, communicating with another subterranean chamber – a sort of second storey to the lower one – but showing no trace of its existence on the surface, as the entrance was carefully concealed by a thick growth of brambles and bracken.

For the initiated, this provided a ready means of access from the outside to the inside of the cavern, which was furnished with steps and platforms, whereby an accomplice above could, by means of a rope, assist those below to climb up, or, if need be, drag up bales of goods for storage in the upper chamber.

As reports began to be whispered thereabouts as to the existence of this Ali Baba's cave, the locality became the scene of fierce struggles between Revenue men and busy smugglers engaged in traffic of contraband.

Time passed and both caves were utterly obliterated during the construction of the railway; but the name of The Brandy Hole is still attached to an inlet in the cliffs, and is now the sole memorial of this smugglers' rendezvous on Bray Head.

In time, the goat track was to become a supply route for those engaged in constructing the new railway around the head. It remains today as part of the cliff walk much enjoyed by now-respectable walkers. The land came under the ownership of Lord Meath.

The same Lord Meath, rather than see the proposed railway laid through the Glen of the Downs, a nearby ravine which was the obvious route for it, gave the present route of the cliff-hugging railway to the venture. For if it had been built through the glen it would have split his estate of Killruddery in two.

Meanwhile, people could walk along the cliff walk for a fee of one penny, payable at a small cottage and gate near The Brandy Hole, except on Fridays, that is, when it was closed for the lord's own use.

Local storyteller Philip Byrne recalled that the gate lodge on the walk was occupied by spinster sisters, one of whom developed a fruit-stall business by Bray railway station, serving the passengers as they travelled to Dublin each day on the newly opened train service.

In no time at all, she caught the attention of one commuter, a dapper businessman, who began to step out with her and soon proposed they be married. The businessman and his bride took up residence in the lodge with the remaining sister who, however, did not take to the smooth-talking gentleman.

Her discomfort with her new brother-in-law eventually led her to follow him into Dublin, where she saw him meet another young lady with whom he entered a hotel, not to emerge until many hours later.

In sorrow, she told her sister of this betrayal.

Rather than engage in reconciliation or discussion on the future path of the sister's marriage, they decided it would be more appropriate to take the life of the wandering man. So, on the following night, the spinster sister delivered a crashing blow to his head with a heavy iron pan, rendering her sibling single once more. They dragged his crumpled body to the low wall overlooking the winding railway track below and tipped him over into the cutting, some 9m below.

At midnight, the sisters were awoken by a terrible moaning coming from the tracks below their cottage, where the body had landed. The undead husband's cries for help continued throughout the long night, but the sisters closed their ears to the sounds.

The early train from Wexford to Dublin passed over him the following morning and in doing so lost a paying customer, for he would commute by train no more.

A subsequent enquiry found that in all likelihood the husband had tripped in the darkness on his way back from the city, fallen over the wall and injured himself on the tracks below. Despite the searching of the sisters during the night, they said, they failed to find him and he had been killed by the 6.35 early train from Wexford.

Many years later, people walking in the area would speak of low moaning sounds in the area of the by then abandoned gate lodge. Perhaps it was sounds from sea creatures, perhaps it was distorted bird call, or perhaps it was something else.

The coming of the railway in the mid-1850s had led to the transformation of Bray and Greystones into fashionable resorts and desirable residential towns. With consultation with Isambard Kingdom Brunel, the celebrated engineer, a single line with several tunnels was constructed and continued round Bray Head and south as far as Wicklow town.

William Dargan, the engineer who was to build nearly 1,000km of railway in Ireland, led the financing and development of the line that snaked around below the toll house. Steps rising up the hill above the toll house led to the Meath estate.

However, from constant erosion, it happened that on 9 August 1867, the train from Enniscorthy to Dublin derailed when it met a faulty joint between two rails on a bridge. Two passengers were killed and twenty-three, including the driver and fireman, were injured.

It proved very difficult to access the crash site to remove people from the area. Following the crash, a new tunnel was built further into the cliff face. The old tunnel entrance can still be seen, a ghost of times past.

Smugglers, lovers and adulterers come and go but Bray Head remains as solid as ever.

25

GOLD-MINE
MOUNTAIN

Somewhere around 1795, gold was officially discovered in the Ballinvalley, otherwise known as the Gold Mines river, a tributary of the river Aughrim, which eventually flows into the sea at Arklow. The Aughrim is a confluence of Derry Water and the River Ow and joins the Avoca downstream of Woodenbridge. These tributary streams may be important, for to this day the mother lode, if it exists, has not been found. Occasional small specks of gold can still be panned by the patient of mind and temperament. However, gold has been found only in pockets in river sand or gravel, or isolated nuggets, or in river drift. Nonetheless, in 2012, a professional prospecting company announced it had found traces of gold on the Wicklow/Wexford border.

Croghan Kinsella, or Gold Mine Mountain, was said to have long been a secret source whence a family named Byrne, resident in its vicinity, derived much benefit. The Gold Mines river flows down a great hollow beneath Croghan Kinsella, or Croghan as the hill became known by those tiring of long titles. Ever since, prospectors have sought gold, using mostly primitive methods, panning river gravels or hunting beneath boulders in the stream for nuggets washed down from the mother lode.

Several large nuggets were found from time to time. One of the biggest pieces took the fancy of the King of England, George IV, during his visit to Ireland in 1821. The monarch absentmindedly,

or otherwise, slipped it into his waistcoat pocket. Royal etiquette forbade the owner to ask for return of his treasure.

Funnily enough, at the time of the first flurry of excitement of discovered gold in Wicklow, in 1795, George was Prince Regent, then a wastrel waiting for his father, Mad King George III – the king who lost America to the rebel army there – to die so that he could succeed to the throne. It was some twenty-six years later that George himself pocketed the gold piece from Wicklow.

The monarch hardly knew or cared about the story of how the gold was first discovered. A schoolmaster, so the story goes, was observed to be very fond of taking solitary walks along the river, especially in the early morning. When asked what he was about, the schoolteacher had replied that he was fishing, no more than that, he said, when pressed for detail. However, most fishermen bring home a fish or two, now or then, or they at least return with a mighty story recalled from their time when there was little to occupy the mind on the bank of the river while waiting for a fish or two to impale itself on a submerged hook.

But no fish did he ever bring home, nor any stories – none worth listening to, at any rate. Nonetheless, the schoolteacher was observed to travel quite regularly to visit the city of Dublin, after which journey he always seemed to have more than enough cash to tide him over until his teacher's pay found its way into his pocket. The trips, as far as anyone could see, had little or nothing to do with his duties as an educator of scholars in his school.

Few secrets remain so for long, for an early morning hiker is easily followed by a discrete pursuer, and Wicklow mountain people can track a living being with the best of them, without being seen. The rambling schoolmaster was eventually seen to take from under a bush not a fishing rod, but the materials of a rocker box, to pan for gold in the river. His secret was discovered and was soon broadcast far and wide. He was panning for gold, and by all account he was finding enough of it to necessitate frequent trips to a Dublin buyer to dispose of his treasure.

Some reports say the secret prospector was a fisherman, not a teacher at all, though there would have been few people – beyond determined and focused poachers – who could have made a living from fishing in the Wicklow mountains.

Within weeks, determined prospectors from many miles around lined the banks of the Gold Mines river, some lying belly down to reach into the water, some standing in the flowing stream, the better to fill up their pans and boxes in search of yellow gold. As always, there was no shortage of older people sitting on their haunches, smoking a pipe and offering advice.

So great did demand become, and so widely did gold fever spread, that workers walked off nearby estates to seek a swift fortune in gold. Presumably, they would then have neither the need nor desire to return to daily employment for another.

Indignant landlords protested that there were no labourers to gather the harvest. Local lore says that laws were passed preventing the searching for gold on working days, lest the crops or the mountain sheep not be tended to as they should be. One account said that as many as 4,000 men, with families in tow, were attracted by the prospect of finding gold for the taking.

During a heady six-week period it was calculated that some 2,666oz or £10,000 worth of ore was collected and sold on by local amateur prospectors, a fortune surely for the best of them at the end of the eighteenth century. The largest piece was said to have weighed 22oz, though whether that was the piece that found its way into George's pocket is hard to say. That piece was said to have been found by one of the Byrne family, who had thought it was copper and used it as a weight, until an itinerant peddler purchased it from him and resold it in Dublin for a large sum.

Indeed, it was reported that the Wicklow gold was so pure that Dublin goldsmiths, when weighing and valuing nuggets, placed a gold coin on the opposite scale and gave weight for weight to the happy prospector.

Croghan is the highest point on the Wicklow-Wexford border, with a tremendous view in clear weather into Wexford county to the south and the rebel Vinegar Hill in the distance. That there was gain to be had from panning for gold in Wicklow was not lost on the government of the day, who moved to take over the profit for the national purse. By law, the Crown claimed a right to any gold found in Ireland.

Thus it was declared that people assembled in the mountains were there for treasonable purposes, and the Kildare Militia was sent to the valley with the double purpose of dispersing the natives and winning the gold. A show of military force made the point that the Crown was now the owner of any wealth so generated and local prospectors were moved out to go elsewhere.

The Irish Parliament, which was to dissolve itself in the 1800 Act of Union, passed a measure to enable the Lords Commissioners of His Majesty's Treasury to conduct the working of a gold mine in Wicklow. Messrs Weaver, Mills and King was appointed to conduct systematic operations, which were carried on until 1798 when the works were destroyed during the rebellion. These agents were instructed to 'endeavour to collect all the gold deposited, and thereby to remove every temptation for the assembling of mobs', which was a neat way of justifying a takeover of any wealth that might be around.

Once private miners were evicted, a large force of workers were recruited, the whole operation being directed by Mr Weaver, the government geologist. Steamworks were established on several rivulets that descended from the mountain; and until May 1798, when work ceased, the total quantity of Treasury gold found was 944oz, or about one-third of that taken up by happy private prospectors in the six weeks before their summary eviction.

While the militia was employed in digging trenches in a search for a lode, locals occupied themselves in prospecting the neighbouring streams. They naturally kept secret any finds, in what had now become a patriotic endeavour. For, in 1798, rebellion having broken out, the troops transferred to Rathdrum barracks, which they fortified with the mining plant from the gold workings.

After the rebellion faded, however, the prospecting agents devoted most of their time to a search for the source of the drift gold in the neighbouring hills, according to a report of a Select Committee on Industries (Ireland) conducted in London, some ninety years later.

In 1801, the mining operations were resumed and works were continued to the heads of the streams. The solid mass of the mountain was more minutely examined, by cutting trenches in every direction down to the firm rock.

The veins discovered by trenching were extensively explored and their depth ascertained by means of a gallery, or level, driven into the mountain at right angles to the general range. But in no instance was a single particle of gold discovered; the result of these operations convinced the government that 'no gold existed as an inherent ingredient in any of the veins which traversed the mountain', the select committee was informed, and the works were consequently abandoned by 1802.

The principal relic of Weaver's workings are the traces of his trenches in a narrow open-cast system, cut across the north-west shoulder of Croghan in an attempt to uncover the mother-lode.

We may only wonder at how much the enterprising schoolteacher managed to lift from the river before the Crown stepped in to ban him from his endeavours, or indeed, how much he and his comrades managed to extract during and after the military occupation of the gold fields of Wicklow.

Following the departure of the Crown prospectors, the locals – or peasants as the authorities were wont to call people – found at least a further £25,000 worth of nuggets in the same stream, according to the select committee report. A further three separate attempts were made in the 1800s to discover the lode, but without success. These failures were attributed to the imperfect and trifling manner in which official operations were carried out, and to the small amount of capital available.

The schoolteacher could have given the authorities lessons in assessing the likelihood of turning a profit from a stretch of Wicklow water, a panning box and an early morning ramble along the banks of a river. Officialdom might have overlooked him, but thousands of ordinary people did not – and many's the peasant's lot that was improved by a visit to the Gold Mine river.

26

PRIEST
HUNTERS

A woman passing an old chapel near Tinahely looked in to say
a prayer, as many people did in a time when churches were left
open all day for worshippers to call in as they chose, Mass being
celebrated in the mornings and devotions being conducted in
the evenings, as a general rule. Yet the story doesn't end there, as
recalled by Michael Hanly of Tinahely to schoolgirl Josie Hanly of
Kevin Street in the same town in the 1930s – a tale now preserved
in the Schools Folklore Collection.

The woman entered the chapel in the afternoon, when she could
reasonably have expected to find the church in quietness. She was
somewhat surprised, then, to see a priest she didn't know saying
Mass at the altar. He was alone; there were no altar servers in attend-
ance as there would normally be. Generally speaking, this would be
a pair of schoolboys, responding to the Latin prayers on behalf of
the congregation by reading from printed cards before them. The
woman soon realised, however, that the celebrant was no living
being. What he was doing there was a mystery to her, although she
felt no fear from being in the presence of a daylight ghost.

As she watched, the ghost turned around to the congregation,
holding his hands out from his body in a priestly gesture. Then
he seemed to realize that there were no servers present. It was a
custom at one time that if the designated servers did not show up,
for an older man who was perhaps a server in his younger days to

take the place and serve the Mass. The ghost shouted out a call for a server: 'Is there no one to serve Mass?' But he was speaking to himself, for he received no answer from the otherwise empty church; the woman had slipped out through the side door beside the mortuary and away to the presbytery, where she fell upon the old iron knocker on the door of the priests' house.

She banged so loudly that she could have woken the dead, if they could have heard her. The parish priests' housekeeper answered the door and, seeing the state the woman was in, admitted her to the hall while she went away to find the priest on duty. The only clergyman available was an older man who was in semi-retirement in the parochial house. He listened to the woman's story, quickly donned a long black coat and stiff black beret and accompanied her to the parish church. As they went in, he blessed himself at the holy water font that stood in the church porch. The woman did likewise, being careful to keep the priest between her and the altar, where the spectral ghost was continuing as best he could with a server-less Mass.

The older man stood at the back of the church for a while. He said nothing, but gestured to the woman to take a seat while he left the building to go around to the vestry behind the altar, where both priest's and server's robes were kept for ceremonies in the church.

The door to the altar opened shortly afterwards and the older priest emerged, dressed in full priestly vestments. He walked around to the foot of the altar steps, bowed to the altar and stepped up to where the ghost priest was hunched over the tabernacle. The older man spoke softly to the spirit for a moment and then stood back, with praying arms extended, as the ghost slowly faded away, never to be seen again in that church.

The older man stayed for a while to say some private prayers before turning to the church in general. He raised his hand in the air and blessed the building and anyone who was in it at that time.

The story is just one of a pair of stories of a ghost priest being seen at Tinahely church. In 1937, Mrs B. Byrne, age 70, of Tinahely told the following story to a Miss Byrne of Kevin Street, Tinahely.

In Penal Days the church was seized by the Crown. Every year thereafter a ghost priest was seen walking around the church. It was said to have been the ghost of a priest hunted and killed by the Driver family, priest-hunters all. Whether true or not, the story said that shortly after the killing, and while the Driver family was eating dinner, one of them choked and died. After which, the rest of the family quickly died off in the area.

Large areas of Wicklow had remained in the control of Irish clans resisting British rule from Dublin. The diocese of Glendalough, which traced itself back to the time of St Kevin, was independent of Dublin until both were amalgamated in 1216. Dublin was administered by an Archbishop that was either of Norman or English origin, so the Irish priests of Glendalough were looked on by the clans and the people as their own.

A 1709 Penal Act demanded that Catholic priests take the Oath of Abjuration, and recognise the Protestant Queen Anne as Queen of the United Kingdom, including Ireland. Priests who did not conform were arrested and executed. Priest hunters were effectively bounty hunters: some were criminals forced into the position by the police; some were volunteers, experienced soldiers or former spies. Not surprisingly, the hunters were viewed as the most despised class in seventeenth- and eighteenth-century Ireland. The Penal Law made fugitives of men of religion. They were forced to conduct services in secret and in remote locations, sometimes at landmark rocks, which to this day are known as Mass rocks. Because the activity was illegal, services were not scheduled, so as to keep the authorities guessing. Their occurrence was communicated by word of mouth among parishioners. As people made their way to the ceremony by way of paths across the hills, others kept watch for pursuers or strangers in the area.

The people sheltered these men of religion for a combination of reasons, including personal religious belief and as resistance to the authority of the government. Nonetheless, the hunted clerics had to be careful of seizure, for a bounty of £10-£20 applied for the capture of a priest. It was such a substantial amount at the time that some were tempted to inform when they knew a priest would be in a certain place at a given time.

Those who were identified as informers against priests put their own life and property at risk. If connivance in the capture of a priest was proven, they faced being burned out of their home and their name vilified by all, for generations.

As for the priests themselves, they hid in what was referred to as 'priest's holes', hiding places built into the big houses of sympathisers that were small spaces behind conventional rooms, safe from prying eyes. Fugitive priests also stayed out on the hills on their own, being fed and cared for by the people.

Such hiding places could take strange turns. A man called Sharkey of Kilcarney recalled a time when a local cave was opened in Penal times as a refuge for priests. The cave was man-made and was situated on the banks of a small river that divides Kilcarney from Rathcoyle.

Locals were cautious at the time that the cave was excavated, for they did not want there to be any signs of the hiding place for priest hunters to see. They waited for the river to flood and began to open up the cave. They dug and dug and threw the hollowed-out clay into the flowing river, where it was quickly swept away in the brown swirling flood, so maintaining the security of the site. However, at times of great rainfall, large floods would sweep down the river, flow over its banks and over the cave and cause it to fall in. It would be rebuilt as soon as possible.

Its use was abandoned in time, but the entrance was to be seen for a long time afterwards to those who wanted to see where the fugitive priests had hidden, placing their lives in jeopardy for the sake of their belief.

But a priest's life sometimes had its amusing side, such as in the following story of a tinker man who decided he wanted to be married by a priest.

He and his woman went up to a priest in the hills and asked him would he wed them for half a sovereign. The sovereign was a gold coin with a nominal value of one pound sterling, which was big money at that time. Nonetheless, the priest said it was a poor price to offer for a marriage by a priest of the one true faith. Perhaps to pass the time and to make the couple come back, the priest said he would wed them surely if they made him a tin can along with the half a sovereign. It was not much to ask, for tinkers were travelling workers in tin and fashioning a can would not overtax them. Such an implement would be very useful to the priest out on the hills to collect drinking and washing water from a passing stream.

The tinker said he would certainly make such a thing and they would return when it was done.

It should not have taken long to fashion the can; however, it was three weeks before they came upon the priest once more. They asked the priest a second time if he would wed them.

'Have you the tin can?' asked the priest.

'We have not', replied the tinker, who went on to explain that he had it made at the fall of night, but the ass gave it a kick that very morning, rending it not fit for the priest at all, and so he had not brought a damaged item with him to offer as an insult to the priest who was going to marry them.

But the priest had seen more in his life than this day and recognised a chancer when he saw one coming, even from a distance of half a mile.

'Go on now', said the priest. 'It's a pair of rogues and schemers you are, and I won't wed you at all.'

The pair argued with him for a while and tried bribery and cajolment in equal measure, to no avail.

They took their leave of him there on the hill and went off; and they were not married afterwards from that day on, whether it was because they were waiting for the priest to change his mind or they thought the price of marriage to be too high.

Such was the life of a fugitive priest, long ago, in between dodging bounty hunters in the Wicklow hills and glens. Indeed, some of them may have become frustrated enough to come back to haunt the place where they died.

27

HEMPENSTALL
MILITARY ROAD

Following the unsuccessful but long-drawn-out rebellion of 1798 the government of the day decreed that a road should be built across the Wicklow Mountains as a swift military access route to subdue recalcitrant rebels. Barracks to house soldiers were built in the glens at Glencree, Laragh, Glenmalure and Aughavannagh.

To link the bases, a regiment of Highland Fencibles was directed in 1799 to camp on the summit of the mountain chain, and begin the task of cutting a road suitable for the movement of soldiers and their equipment, from the village of Rathfarnham in southern Dublin to the barracks of Aughavannagh, many miles south across the mountains. They were paid a shilling a day for their troubles, according to the records.

Nonetheless, by the time the road reached the barracks at Aughavannagh, the most southerly of the military strongpoints, Dwyer and his rebels had given up, and had been transported beyond the seas to exile in Australia.

To this day, the road the soldiers built passes through wild mountain areas, where nothing is to be seen but commonage and bog. Pretty in summer, in winter it is inhospitable, raw and life-threatening for the unwary, the inhabitants of which are wild animals and the undomesticated fowl of the hills.

Sedges and bog-cotton are a feature of the waterlogged granite grounds, with heather and furze sprouting on the better drained areas of schist. While the fencibles toiled at their roadmaking we may suppose that the rebels lay and watched them and wondered why so much effort should be spent on building a road across bog in order to deter Wicklow men from fighting for the right to live as they chose.

But the road, before it was finished, was to bring the rule of martial law and summary execution to the glens. A killer called Hempenstall came to be identified as the public face of military cruelty.

The road rises at Rathfarnham in the suburbs of Dublin. It crosses the Featherbeds and skirts the head of Glencree, where the first barracks was built, and a spur road was run down to Enniskerry. The complex is now a reconciliation centre. The military route arrived at Sally Gap, one of the two highest passes in the county, before descending past the white-watered Glenmacnass waterfall to Laragh, rising again to descend to Glenmalure and Drumgoff Barracks, now in ruins, and up and down once more to the barracks of Aughavannagh, still standing, where the executioner Hempenstall was to meet his own entirely unexpected end, one dark night when help was not at hand.

Wicklow glens have run from east to west for 500 million years or so, yet the direction of the eighteenth-century road is north to south, making its construction a challenge for the military engineers tasked with its construction. Their difficulty in marking out the line of road advantageously may be judged by the modern traveller who is now served by a hard modern road surface running along the original route of the road.

As recently as 100 years ago, the road beyond Sally Gap, which at almost 500m is Ireland's highest crossroads, could be made impassable because of soft going following rain, which falls as part of a day's routine weather in the hills of Wicklow.

Until the early 1950s, this part of the road had become practically derelict, having had few major repairs since its construction. It was even deleted from several maps, as a consequence, until Wicklow County Council undertook major work to bring it back to an acceptable standard. Even the road along the Featherbeds, where many Dubliners cut home turf during the Emergency, was gouged away in places by heavily laden lorryloads of turf in the 1939-45 period.

Nowadays, in more peaceful times, at springtime plumes of smoke can be seen rising from the hills, where sheep-men burn off heather and furze to extend their grazing. Ash from the burnings falls on the soil and is soon turned into fertiliser by soft mountain rains. Sometimes, in hot dry periods rebellious fires spread to threaten the pervasive State forests that marched over the hills in the twentieth century.

However, at the end of the eighteenth century, existence was harsher for people in the Wicklow Mountains, where life was lived at a basic subsistence level by many. Few, outside of the rebels, would have been concerned about the approach of a road for soldiers to move along, beyond noting where it was on any given day. They would have been more deeply concerned with the harshness of the same soldiers' superiors in dealing with what they declared to be disloyalty among the populace. Since martial law was the order of the day, the normal rights of citizens could be put at naught.

One of the most terrifying characters of the period was the hangman: Jack Hempenstall. He is said to have stood over 7ft tall at a time when the average Wicklow person may not have been much higher than a pair of feet below the towering hangman.

Justice and punishment at the time did not include long stays in prison at the government's expense. Floggings, fines, deportations and hangings saw those found guilty moved quickly through the system of retribution.

Faced with the severity of martial law, few would care to find themselves in the presence of the looming Hempenstall, who was a member of the Wicklow militia and frequented the Aughavannagh area, in particular. He held sway in the south-facing barracks that occupies a strategic position near two road junctions on the Military Road, with panoramic views in all directions.

A pair of towers flanked the three-storey ten-bay barrack block. From the top of the towers, watchers could see activity in any direction and react accordingly, by sounding the alarm. The barracks area was surrounded by stone walls from where defenders could fire at any approaching attackers. An entrance gateway was surmounted by a stone archway through which those with business passed in or out of the barracks precinct.

A favoured form of interrogation of the time was to half-hang a suspect during questioning. The victim was hauled up off their feet by a noose around the neck as if to be hanged to death. But just as all expectation had faded and they had given up hope of life, they were lowered once more to recover their breath and sensibilities.

The interrogation would begin all over again, when the victim was supposedly weakened by his or her terrifying experience and their resolve was sorely lessened. It was Hempenstall's particular refinement of this torture to place the noose around his victim's neck and raise him up himself. He carried a rope in his saddle bag for just such a purpose. He would snake the free end of the rope over his own broad shoulder and hoist the protesting and thrashing unfortunate high up on his back. If they gave in to the interrogation they then found themselves lying on the ground at Hempenstall's boots, ready to tell all, however unwillingly. If it was to be an execution, he walked about and held the person there until they had quietened. With a twist of his wrist he broke their neck, ending their suffering forever. For this, he rejoiced in the title of the walking hangman among rebel and loyalist alike. He was admired, feared and hated by those who came across him. To this day, his name is recalled with a mixture of anger, disdain and loathing.

Hempenstall was to meet his death at the hands of those he tormented. His own demise was every bit as violent as those actions he had for so long meted out to so many helpless captives who came into his charge. Various versions of the story of his death say he was killed in some unspecified way, or he was knifed, or he was shot at the gateway of the barracks in Aughavannagh and died on the spot.

However, a recent telling in Aughavannagh by the descendant of one he had terrorised said that Hempenstall was piked at the gateway to the barracks one night. It was said in such a positive and matter-of-fact way that it recalled the first reports that must have spread though the glen when news passed one to another that the rebels had caught up with the walking hangman, who would hang no more without judge or jury to hear the victim's case.

The killers had used the long-handled weapons favoured by the insurrectionists that allowed a distance to be kept from the quarry while inflicting the deadliest of wounds. Determined and experienced pike users operating in concert could have faced and killed the largest of wild animals when they had it cornered. The towering figure of Hempenstall was cornered and piked to death at the gateway to the barracks from where he had himself spread so much quaking terror.

As time passed and the building ceased to have any use as a military station and the troops moved out, it was used for some time as a shooting lodge by Charles Stewart Parnell, leader of the constitutional Irish Parliamentary Party.

After Parnell's death, it was taken over by John Redmond, a leading Parnellite, who used it as a residence. In his time, the house supported a staff of some thirty people. Locals recall shooting visits by Redmond's friend, Tim Healy, a former Parnellite and the first governor-general of the Irish Free State.

The old gateway still stands today, in its remote and now peaceful setting, much as it was on the turbulent evening when the walking hangman met rough justice at the hands of the friends and comrades of those who had found no mercy in Hempenstall.

It is there, at the gateway that became so familiar to so many visitors when the old barracks became a youth hostel, that there have been frequent reports of the presence of a frightening figure. Many say it is the ghost of the hangman himself.

Some reported that when walking towards the gate in pitch darkness on a moonless night, a dragging noise behind them in the all-enveloping blackness made them quicken their step towards the warm yellow light spilling from the open wooden doorway of the old barracks.

Is it Hempenstall, dragging a dying victim on his back, until all is silent once more? Or, is it the sighing sound of a human's last breath as life so ignominiously leaves their protesting body? Or is it nature commenting on the follies of men?

Whatever causes the prickling sensation on the lonely road, many people say, with some determination, that the old Aughavannagh barracks is haunted by the ghost of a hangman. It would be a determined person indeed who would challenge the belief by venturing into the pervasive darkness of this remote Wicklow glen, alone and on foot.

28

WICKLOW
AVALANCHE

The winter of 1867 saw very severe weather all over Ireland. Snow fell everywhere, and deeply, especially in the Wicklow Mountains. By late March, Wicklow (both low and high) was covered in snow, with many roads washed away by melting snow and snowdrifts still blocking the high passes.

A marked feature of Irish snowfall is its variation in depth from place to place. Even heavy snowfalls can be quite localised. Then again, drifts of 6m or more have been reported in hill areas, bringing torment to those caught up in its effects.

The higher reaches of Wicklow Mountains have an average snowfall of up to thirty days in a year, with depths of 1cm or more accruing in the year, according to Met Eireann, the national weather service.

Tragedy fell in 1867 when, during the daylight hours of 23 March, following heavy and persistent snowfall, a thaw began. Floods formed quickly on the hills and flowed downstream. Ferocious flooding in the glens led to the destruction of life, of homes, roads and bridges. A stone bridge was in part washed away. Onlookers standing on a remaining section had to jump to safety when the rest of the structure joined the cascading floodwaters beneath where they had recently stood.

Floodwaters carried away poor people's homes. Many were simply demolished by the force of water, others joined the flood as so much jetsam. Trees and brushwood swept downstream like small matches bobbing in the brown water, vying for position.

According to local newspapers of the day, at Drumgoff, Glenmalure, two children lost their lives when the miner's hut they called home was swept away. One was taken from the water dead, another was not discovered until later. A third girl was badly injured and was expected to die as a result. At Lough Dan, a woman and two children were carried away by a mountain torrent after the sudden thawing of 3m of snow and the heavy rains that arrived on Saturday 23 March. On the same Saturday forenoon, at Inchavon at the head of Lough Dan, 4 miles from Roundwood, moving snow took away cabins where sheep and cattle had been placed for protection. Another tragedy struck at the Smith home. With the avalanche descending towards the Smith house, someone who saw what was happening shouted a warning to Mrs Smith. She had a child in her arms at the time. She rushed to save another child in her house and all three were buried in 2.5m of snow, just metres from their home. Their bodies were not recovered from the snow for several hours, despite strenuous efforts.

The torrent coming through Glenmalure along the Avonbeg river was like Powerscourt waterfall in ferocity, said people who were there on the day and saw it. Miraculously, a baby in a floating cot was found to be safe by rescuers, but the infant's mother was lost in the flood. Miners' cottages built under the gorge by the lead mining company for their workers were totally swept away.

In Glencree, further north, some 200 'delinquent' boys who had been sentenced to detention in Glencree Reformatory by the courts, many for petty transgressions, were turned out by their guardians to help clear away the effects of the floods, as the extent of the devastation became apparent. The reformatory was housed in the former military barracks. At that time, all supplies for the reformatory had to be brought over the Military Road from Dublin, to the north. However, that road was frequently blocked by snowdrifts during winter. For the most part, the boys were sickly, undernourished and in bad health.

On the coast, fishermen were kept ashore by dreadful weather and were unable to venture out to earn a living. Those families that relied on income from casual work were in dire straits, for most normal commerce was disrupted because of foul weather. Inland floods swirled everywhere that water could find a course to follow.

In Arklow, the parish priest James Redmond reported that in his parish alone some 500 families received relief of two shillings per family that week to help alleviate their distress. Further along the coast, the railway between Kingstown and Dalkey was under water for a time as the sea poured in and floodwaters cascaded down from the hinterland. Nonetheless, according to contemporary accounts, the flood level was not high enough to put out the engine fires and so trains continued to run, where possible.

The *Bray Gazette* reported earlier that month that the British Electric Telegraph Company had been granted permission to extend its new telegraph service between Bray and Roundwood. Wooden poles to carry the wires were to be bought locally from the estate of Earl Fitzwilliam and local labourers were to be hired for the duration of the works. However, all such effort halted as floods swept through Wicklow.

Sometime during the night, the partially melted snow on the hills began to move in places, as trickling melt water provided a custom-made slide for its progress. Complete tragedy was to visit an entire family living beneath the brow of Shielstown Hill in the parish of Askanagap. Residents of nearby houses reported hearing a sound like the distant rumble of thunder and then all was still once more. All over as swiftly as it had begun.

The Mulhall family lived in a cabin, or cottage, a short distance above a stream and near a mountain track that led on up Shielstown Hill. From the cottage, there is a stiff climb north to the summit of the hill. It happened that the ground overlooking the Mulhall homestead could not curtail the weight of the newly fallen snow as it began to move, once a thaw began. Local commentators reported that an avalanche of snow slid down the precipitous hill and levelled the young family's home. The entire family, six in number, were lost.

The family not having made their appearance at noon on the following day, neighbours feared something had happened and made a search. They removed snow from where the cabin should have stood and rolled away large stones that had been washed down the hill with the avalanche in the night. Unexpectedly, they found all the family members lying in bed as if in a quiet sleep. Each had expired under the avalanche, smothered in soft white snow in their sleep.

The bodies of James Mulhall, his wife Kate and their children, Brian aged 7, Peter aged 5, Mary aged 3 and baby James aged 14 days, were removed to a neighbour's house and the authorities were notified of their sudden death.

Inquests and inquiries moved faster in those times than today. An inquest, on the same day, by Phillips Newton Esquire, the coroner for the Askanagap part of Wicklow, made a finding in accordance with evidence as given, and the case was closed.

Today only the low walls of the house remain on the site, offering a sheltered spot for walkers who pause to read the plaque erected in memory of the sleeping family, at the place where they retired together in repose on a snowy night in Wicklow in 1867. The family is also commemorated by a public notice at Preban graveyard, near Tinahely, to where the bodies were taken after the inquest, and interred.

The family were buried in the graveyard of Preban church, an early medieval ecclesiastical site, whose main features are traces of an old church surrounded by a graveyard. Sadly, for the moment, no gravestone stands above the last resting place of the Mulhalls, but each year, in July, a modern blessing of the graves takes place at Preban.

Oddly enough, the late Wicklow walker J.B. Malone recorded that a party of mountaineers staying in a mountain hut in the Cairngorm Mountains in Scotland were killed when their house was crushed by an enormous mass of snow sliding down the hillside at almost the same time as the Mulhall family perished.

The Scottish group's resting place was covered over by snow pouring down an almost exactly similar flat-topped, steep sided hill. It took away their lives as surely as it did the sleeping Mulhall family on a Wicklow hillside.

29

GLENCREE

By modern standards it is difficult to contemplate the imprisonment of a child in a former military barracks at the head of a
Wicklow glen for the purpose of reforming the child's behaviour. But throughout the nineteenth century this was exactly
what happened. Under the Irish Reformatory Schools' Act,
a judge, police magistrate or justice of peace at petty sessions was
empowered to send to a reformatory school any young offender
aged up to 19 years.

To make matters even more terrifying for the youngster, he or
she had to be first sentenced to imprisonment for at least fourteen
days. Such imprisonment was to be passed in strict solitary con-
finement. In the case of Glencree Reformatory, this meant that all
boys (it was an institution for boys only) were first housed in a cell
in Kilmainham Gaol in Dublin.

Kilmainham was a secure prison where adult revolutionaries and
others were incarcerated and where, in 1916, the leaders of the failed
Easter Rising were officially shot, executed under martial law.

For the boys sent to the reformatory, that the term of their
detention should not be less than three nor more than five years
must have been cold comfort. Some idea of the severity of conditions is reflected in the stipulation that the boy should be free
from any constitutional infirmity that would render him unfit for
industrial training.

Nonetheless, for the most part, the boys were sickly, undernourished and in bad health when they arrived at the reformatory. So much so, that on arrival they were taken in over a ramp at the rear, rather than through the gates, where they would have been in contact with others. They were then held again in isolation, this time in Glencree, where they were deloused before entering the general populace to begin their period of State-approved reform.

In the month of February 1870, just three years after the heavy snowfall and avalanches of 1867, one youngster, Bernard Young, sentenced for the crime of petty larceny in Belfast, died from exposure during heavy snowdrifts on Featherbed Mountain on the way to Glencree. The road there is windswept and bare and meanders across dark-brown peat bogland where even the green grass is frost-burnt red in winter.

All other places of detention in the country were full and it was finally agreed by Glencree that they would hold him in Wicklow, many kilometres from his hometown to the north. He was dressed in rags and was barefoot on the journey that passed by the hulk of the Hell Fire Club on Dublin's mountains and continued along the road as its jurisdiction passed from Dublin to Wicklow authorities. Local folklore says that his guards stopped at a shebeen on the way across the windswept road, leaving the boy outside in the piercing cold to fend for himself, to shelter as best he might. Dunnes of the Hill was the name of the shebeen, which stood less than 1km away from the warmth and safety of the towering walls of the reformatory. The guards went in to drink while 12-year-old Bernard Young was left outside in his restraining chains, where he perished.

However, the official report into the boy's death does not mention a shebeen stop, saying instead that the weather being very inclement, he perished in a snowstorm on the mountain while being taken from Dublin to the reformatory. The report does not say that the guards also perished from the same cause, as they did not.

The original Glencree barracks was designed to accommodate a captain and 100 soldiers. By 1870, with additional capacity, it housed 325 boys, 3 priests and 19 religious brothers, together with lay staff. In that year, two boys absconded from the reformatory but were quickly recaptured, according to the official report.

Twenty-seven years later, boys were still trying to get away from the reformatory. According to other official reports of the time, two boys succeeded in making their escape in 1897, but they were captured and brought back during the year. There was also, in May, a desperate attempt on the part of three 'unsatisfactory' boys to get away from one of the farm batches, but the boys were secured and brought back before they had got very far. What was 'unsatisfactory' about them, we can but wonder.

That year, the death was reported of two boys who, after changeable and very trying weather towards the close of the year, fell sick and succumbed to pneumonia. One of them had always been extremely delicate, and both were born deformed, said the annual report for the year.

A memorial cross was erected in Bernard Young's name, where the shebeen once stood, but has since vanished. Some say that it disappeared, others say that someone has possession of it, without being specific as to who that might be, or why it was removed, or what is to happen to it.

Perhaps it was removed for safety around the time that the neighbouring statue of the Good Shepherd was taken from a nearby location above the road. The memorial statue to the religious order that ran Glencree became the target of some confused marksman who used it for target practice. It was eventually taken down, in sorrow. Before that, it had been a landmark of sorts to those crossing the high road in mist that often covers the mountainside above Glencree, on the way to Sally Gap and places south.

An evergreen holly bush planted in 1940 when the reform school was removed to Daingean in Co. Offaly has fared better. Birds are said never to take the red fruit from the tree, which was planted in memory of the boys and staff who passed some of their life there. The holly bush grows there still.

Boys were trained in the reformatory as cabinetmakers, upholsterers, carvers, turners, carpenters, smiths and fitters, painters, stonecutters, quarriers and masons, tailors and shirtmakers, shoemakers and harnessmakers, bakers, farmyard boys, gardeners, horse followers, farm labourers, or laundry boys. The youngest boys were taught to knit. Others worked in the dormitory, lavatory, infirmary, kitchen and refectory, some as houseboys, and others in charge of the gas works and steam boiler. There was even a band that stood in a circle outdoors and played on occasions for the assembled ranks of other boys. It is not certain how many went on to work at their new trades, for on release there was no follow-on support available for them.

Their uniform in the school was a brown tweed tunic; drab moleskin vest and trousers; a striped coloured shirt; a flannel vest during the cold season; a black cloth Glengarry cap and Blucher boots. Their diet was selected from a basic ration of bread, tea, cocoa, oatmeal stirabout, meat soup, vegetable soup, meat and potatoes – though not all on the same day.

Some wrote back from wherever they subsequently found themselves in life, most did not. One wrote from Butte City, Montana, to say he was getting along fine but had to look out for himself as he was in a mining camp, and a pretty lawless one at that. Another was in Eshowe, Zululand, where he said he was in the British Army there and could only get to Mass once every three months because there were no trains running. Another was elsewhere in Wicklow, working every day in a Protestant house where the wages were very low. He was unhappy and asked to be told of anyone who wanted a good boy to work with them.

Water was sourced for the complex from a natural spring well on the mountain behind the reformatory. But just one tap was allowed per building, in the interest of continuity and equity of supply. And so they existed.

The building was empty again once the reformatory moved to Offaly, but during the Emergency it was occupied by members of the Civilian Construction Corps, which existed between 1940 and 1948, who cut turf, improved the mountain roads and helped farmers.

By 1942, when all that remained of the boys were silent memories, the condition of the Featherbed Road was raised in a Dáil Éireann debate when the Minister for Local Government and

Public Health was asked if he was aware that the road was almost impassable, and so it would not be possible to remove turf that was being cut in the area. Minister MacEntee said that quantities of stone were being hauled over the road in preparation for steam-rolling. The road was naturally in poor condition owing to the transport of stone. It was being temporarily patch-rolled so as to keep it in fair order as the actual reconstruction proceeded, he said.

In happier times, at the end of the Emergency from 1945 onwards, Glencree rang with merriment and hesitant laughter as it became a temporary refugee centre under the auspices of the Irish Red Cross. The French Sisters of Charity cared for thousands of German and Polish war orphans on UN-sponsored three-month rest programmes or en route to longer-stay fostering in Irish homes. Glencree was used as a reception and settling-in centre for children from the battlefield of Europe before they were placed in the care of foster families throughout Ireland.

Operation Shamrock resettled more than 1,000 children, some as young as 3 years old, from war-torn Germany, Austria and France. Most were later repatriated to their homelands, but some were readily adopted by their Irish host families. Some fifty German children remained in Ireland and eventually married Irish partners. In 2013, a reunion and commemoration of Operation Shamrock was scheduled for Glencree as part of 'The Gathering', an Ireland-wide initiative to encourage people to visit Ireland.

In the present century, a man called Paddy, a recovering alcoholic, found his way to the church in the reformatory grounds built where once the main kitchen stood. Saying his private prayers, he believed that a statue of Our Lady spoke to him and asked for a Mass to be said there every month so that Glencree would become known as a place of peace.

He relayed this request to the priest, who agreed to celebrate a special Mass on the first Saturday of the following month, which continues to this day. The first Mass was said when there was snow on the ground. Strangely enough, attendees remarked afterwards that there was a scent of roses while the Mass was being said, taken to be a sign of Our Lady's presence, according to local folklore.

Nearby, in a declivity beside the Glencree river, at this point just a healthy stream tumbling over lichen-covered rocks of all sizes, is a Marian grotto that has become a place of quiet pilgrimage for many. Some people leave mementoes at the grotto, built below the level of the road, and pray for their intentions. Others, whose homes are in faraway lands in central Europe, come here to pray for deceased members of their family where they cannot return to the loved ones resting place.

For many, Glencree has become a final resting place of peace.

30

SURVIVING THE
SNOW STORM

Wicklow in summer is the loveliest place, with its bog-covered rolling hills, verdant pastures, silent glens and the gentle waves that caress its shores to the east. It can be the resort of the idle, the playground of the rich, the wonder of the visitor and the happy home of the native, rambling its boreens and mountain passes as generations have done before, with the fragrance of summer bog all around.

In olden times, tinkers and tramps walked its roads on the way to or from somewhere or another. Many wanderers merely drifted away from the ordinary people of the villages. Although fallen on hard times, they were nevertheless quite similar in outlook and temperament to the people they passed in the houses on the side of the road.

Red-coated soldiers once marched along the high Military Road that winds over the hills in endless search for the long departed United Irishmen rebels.

All said, Wicklow can present a bucolic appearance to the visitor travelling along.

Nevertheless, once the seasons change and snow tumbles down and winter closes is grip on the countryside, the same hills and valleys can become a most forbidding place, where life and limb may be lost by the unwary or the foolish. Stock or man can vanish and be found long afterwards, accidentally or only by determined searchers, perhaps found only as a rotten carcass on the side of the hill, pecked to bits by carrion crow.

Bad weather is often predicted: goats return home when a storm is expected and will enter the kitchen of the house if not chased away. Mountain hares gather in a bunch when it is about to snow. White-backed sheep keep low down on the hills, the woolly quadrupeds lie along the ditch for shelter when bad weather approaches.

At such times, the whistling wind has teeth in it and the older countyman will sense that snow is on its way. To the mountain men, a winter wind from the south-east signals bitterly cold weather on the way.

But for all the warning signs little can be done by man to forestall nature when it moves to blanket the countryside in silent, deadly snow.

In the north of the county, a monument was erected dating back to 1804, when a snowstorm caught a rider and his horse out on the hill. The rider's name was Beahs and he ended his mortal life in the chilling snowstorm in that year. According to the story, both horse and rider were overwhelmed in a deep snowdrift on the side of the road. Unable to free either himself or his horse, both man and animal perished from exposure, just a few miles away from the warmth and lights of the capital city of Dublin to the north-east.

Outdoor clothing in the nineteenth century was not such as to withstand prolonged exposure to a chilling wind, and loss of body heat could quickly lead to hypothermia and death if rescue did not arrive in time. A rescue party that battled its way through the drifts in search of the missing man discovered both horse and rider stiff and lifeless the next day.

The stone cross monument to Patrick Beahs was erected a couple of kilometres across a boggy mountain tract near Ballyfolan, where the road sweeps to the right and enters grassy country, which is where he met his chilling end. Summer walkers to this spot find it difficult to believe that death from hypothermia was caused here by a simple snowstorm.

But the silent onset of snow in the mountains, covering over everything, has fooled more than one traveller. When it comes, snow will penetrate every chink and cranny of the hills, cover every track and trail with as much menace as it did to those first people who came into what is now Wicklow on the tail of the Ice Age.

Severe frost will cause great blocks of rock to split. As it did once, causing rock to fall from the cliffs of Ben Leagh and Ben Dooagh, sliding down the snow banks beneath the cliffs to form rock piles like the moraines of the Alpine glaciers of continental Europe.

The snow may melt as soon as it falls, or it may linger for ages afterwards high up at the top of the Wicklow or Sally Gap or on Percy's Table on looming Lugnaquilla. If the snow is followed by a severe frost, many people may be snowbound for long periods while a thaw is awaited.

Such was the weather in January 1982 when a sudden snowfall left many glens isolated. Three intense snowstorms covered the whole island in white for the best part of three weeks. A thirty-six-hour blizzard began on 7 January, effectively closing down road transport where drifts obliterated roads and made journeys impossible. Two more falls over the following ten days saw local snowfalls join forces with snow showers drifting in from the Irish Sea, adding to the drifts across Wicklow that by then had already frozen and compacted on the ground.

Residents of Aughavannagh were cut off and were pleased to see an Irish army helicopter eventually arrive over the southern valley to drop feeding for livestock and emergency supplies for the farmers of the area. On-board was a local garda from Aughrim who was expected to know where each family lived and whose task it was to guide the crew over their homes and to ensure that all that could be done was done.

Still, it was not as bad as the snow of 1947, which has entered the collective memory of the Irish people as the Great Snow that lasted on the ground in some places until April of that year. It began on 25 February and was recorded as the greatest single snowfall to have visited Wicklow and the other counties on the island. It was said by those who lived through it to have snowed continuously for fifty consecutive hours. The 1947 storm was driven by persistent easterly gales that came across the frozen lands of Europe to turn snow into white ice everywhere.

An even earlier snow in the same century became the subject of a strange occurrence when a man went in search of his lost brother and found him in extraordinary circumstances.

Michael O'Byrne, who was aged 50 at the time, and who lived in Cronawinna, Aughrim, told primary-school pupil Eddie O'Byrne that unexpected snow fell overnight in February 1933. It started at 5 o'clock in the evening, just after darkness had settled, and continued through the night.

Snow had been threatening all day and anyone with an eye in their head could see what was about to happen. It began to fall steadily in small heavy flakes and eventually amounted to drifts of almost 3m in depth, said local man Thomas Caulfield.

The snow was piled up against people's kitchen doors on the first morning, making exit from their houses very hard to achieve. People dug their way out with small coal shovels, a little at a time, Michael O'Byrne recalled for the younger lad, who wrote it all down as part of a school exercise.

To make matters worse, few sheep owners had taken in their animals, despite the warning signs of the day before.

People dug paths down their lanes and to the road gates to try to connect with neighbours and make a way to bring in emergency supplies wherever they could source them. That done, and the immediate pressures relieved in homesteads, men went in search of lost sheep. The searchers' chests became sore from the coldness of the air as they breathed in the snow-swept atmosphere around them.

They poked long poles, 7m long, into the snow to find buried sheep. Everywhere was glaring bright from the whiteness of the snow. Sheepdogs smelt for sheep beneath the snow, sniffing deep into the holes made by the men with their poles. If they found something then the sheepmen dug down in search of life.

But since the snow was very deep, many landmarks were rendered useless as a guide to where the sheep would have been thought to have naturally gathered. A buried four-strand fence of wire above a usually familiar ditch might not even be visible to the eye. The work was long and arduous and sapped the men's strength and resolve.

In addition to the probing poles, the dogs would discover occasional air holes kept open by the warm breath of ewes trapped beneath the snow. There, the men dug with frozen hands, beeling fingers and soaking clothes and footwear. They dragged the helpless beasts by the shoulders out of the holes.

The search continued into the second and third day. Few mountain men wore more than the normal clothes that anyone wore in those days. The only concession to the season would be a few more layers worn over the undergarments and a well-pulled-down cap or an old hat.

The 1933 snow lasted for three weeks. In the end it finished up with a heavy night's rain washing away the lingering snow into the mountain streams to flood them once more on their way out to the waiting sea.

But before this happened, the houses around Macreddin were covered over with white precipitation. An old man in Macreddin took to his legs to see if his brother, a bachelor who lived in another house, was alive and surviving the depredations of the hard winter. However, it was not long before the old man lost his way in the snow.

It was said that the snow in places rose up to the tops of the trees, though it was not said what height the tress actually were, whether they had been growing for many years and had achieved height in maturity or whether they were saplings in the new State forest, feeling their way to the sky for the first time.

In any case, the old man saw a depression a little way from him in the ground. There was a wisp of something rising up from it, he noted. It might be a sheep, he thought, and made for it.

Imagine then his surprise to see that the hole in the snow was about 0.5m wide and that the wisp he saw from afar was a wisp of smoke.

It was turf smoke, he could tell by the tang of it, good hard turf as well, the sort favoured by his brother.

He approached as close as was safe and looked down.

If he was shocked to see smoke rising from the snow where he thought he had found a sheep's breath, he was even more surprised to see who was looking back up at him.

It was a face that was familiar and dear to him, the face of his brother staring back at him.

'I was looking for you', he said.

'You found me so', replied his brother in a good clear voice.

'What are you doing there in a hole?' asked the old man with interest.

'I'm sitting at my own fire. You're standing on my roof and looking down the chimney. Be careful you don't fall off the roof', said his brother. 'I can't get out in the snow to help you if you do.'

The searcher looked around and could see no undulation in the landscape that would show he was standing on a roof or standing in the yard.

'Do you want me to come down and help you out?' he asked uncertainly.

'No,' said the brother, 'I have the two goats in here with me and I sold the sheep last month, so I'll stay where I am until the snow goes. I have plenty of turf in. I'll be warm enough. I'm looking at stories here in the ashes of the fire in the grate and wondering what they mean. Will you find your way home safe?'

'I will', said his brother, and made his way back through the snow, following his own footsteps in reverse until he was as safe in his own house as his brother was in his.

And so he remained, until the thaw came in its own good time and he could go rambling with dry feet once more.

31

TALL
TALES

The earliest people to come to Ireland arrived some 9,000 years ago by boat, or so early storytellers relate. Coastal areas were inhabited before any others. The early settlers moved inland along the rivers using the transport they knew best. At that time Ireland, including Wicklow, was covered in deep forests, down to the water's edge.

Within these forests was a ready supply of deer and wild pig to be hunted for meat, while there was an abundance to be had of wild fruits and nuts to supplement the diet of working people making their way in a new land.

Wicklow rivers abounded in salmon and trout; while along the seashore sea animals and shellfish were to be found aplenty. But there were also bears and wolves that in turn could eat people and, until St Patrick came and hunted them out, an amount of snakes caused some nuisance to barefooted travellers.

However, the settlers did not build large houses or burial tombs to remember them by and so archaeological evidence of their life and times is difficult to find. In which case, to know something of the early Irish, we rely on folklore and stories handed down one to another through the generations.

Most stories are factual, if a little embellished, but trouble arises when the original teller of the story was confused or was a fanciful fool, for when it came time around the campfire to tell a story, it was not acceptable to say that 'nothing unusual occurred that day, perhaps tomorrow'. A story had to be told to the waiting listeners to inform, persuade or entertain. Thus it was that many tall tales found their way into the folklore canon.

That habit of telling a story to while away the time has continued up to the present day. And the same problem arises when a real story is not readily to hand and a fantasy is included out of politeness to the listener. So, listeners find themselves being wary of tall tales told solemnly by a pure-born liar. They enjoy them, but take them as they would their roasted wild boar, with a pinch of salt.

For instance, Fionn Mac Cumhaill, is said to sleep in a hidden place surrounded by the Fianna. It is said that the day will come when his hunting horn, the Dord Fiann, will sound three times and Fionn and the Fianna will rise up again, as strong and well as they ever were, to free Ireland once more.

Speed the day.

However, while the motif of a slumbering chieftain awaiting only arousal to restore glory is an international one, the idea of Fionn and the lads sleeping in your granny's back field takes some believing. That, however, does not stay the tongue of local storytellers up and down the country, who will testify that this is indeed the case.

A storyteller identified only as Mr Fleming of Corballis in Rathdrum told a young story collector back in the mid-1930s that there was a tunnel a couple of kilometres outside Rathdrum at Stump Castle, now ruined. This underground tunnel, he said, led from the old castle to Avondale, the home of Charles Stuart Parnell, the fallen chieftain of the Irish people.

Not only that, but anybody who went in did not come out, so a mystery was added to a secret. That is, until an inebriated gentleman of the locality stumbled into the entrance. Somewhat confused, the man entered the dark tunnel and travelled a distance along it. He was surprised to find a mighty army there. But far from being a bustling encampment, with figures moving here and there, both men and horses were fast asleep. Unsurprisingly, the drunken gentleman cried out in fear, for what else could he do

under the circumstances, for he was surely where he should not have been, and quite possibly in personal danger.

In response to his exclamation, men and horses began to show signs of waking. The leader, a man taller than all of the others, drew his sword and enquired with a loud shout: 'Has the time come?' But the intruder quietly assured him that it was not time yet. Whereupon all settled down once more into their long hiatus and the gentleman made his way to safety as expeditiously as he could.

Tradition has it that if the visitor answered yes, it was time, the army would rise up and battle to free Ireland. But, according to the story, the visitor did not, and instead staggered home as best he could to his own bed.

We can be sure that this story relates to Fionn Mac Cumhaill and the Fianna, or similar, for although the tunnel allegedly runs into Parnell's home place, Parnell was a leader of a constitutional nationalist movement and unlikely to have an army of warriors sleeping on the grounds, awaiting the day. Besides, Parnell was buried in Glasnevin Cemetery in Dublin, in 1891. His interment was attended by more than 200,000 people. His gravestone is of unhewn Wicklow granite, and reads only 'Parnell'.

Not to be outdone in the matter of unusual apparitions at Stump Castle, or the Stump of the Castle as some refer to the ruins, a Mrs Kelly of Lower Street in Rathdrum told a story of a servant who worked in the place when it was a bona fide castle.

The servant looked out of a window in the castle at midnight. It must have been a moonlit night for what she saw there would need some light shone upon it.

For she reported that she saw a hearse drawn by four black head-less horses. It was a *cóiste bodhar*, a death coach. What was more, the driver of the horses was also headless. To attest to this occurrence, it was said that the wheel marks of the hearse are there yet. Or, at least, they were there in 1937 when this story was related as truthful. They may not be there now; but who knows what might be found by wandering around in the dark of the night in the environs of Rathdrum, Co. Wicklow, inebriated or uninebriated.

For all that, people will retell stories in good faith even if the original storyteller did not hew all that close to the essential truth of the story.

Michael Byrne, a 50-year-old farmer of Ballynaghol, Knockanna, averred that Moll Anthony who lived in Arklow was a witch. It was stated by several people that Moll had a clear knowledge of things long hidden and to come. On several occasions, she was consulted by people who had lost the profits and who had no butter on their milk. In every case she stated that a neighbour had taken it.

Her remedy was to take the collar of a plough and put it into the fire. Whoever entered the house when the collar was red hot had their profit. This was done and the perpetrator was caught, according to the story told in Wicklow (the same story is told about Biddy Early, who dwelt on the far side of the country in Co. Clare).

What put the cap on the series of Arklow stories was that a priest denounced the wise woman, whereupon his horse fell down and could not get back up again until Moll Anthony shook her apron at him and the horse rose up, after which the priest said no more about her. The self-same story is told of Biddy Early.

And there is the minor matter of Kildare claiming the same Moll as their own. Moll Anthony is said to have passed away in

1878. She was reputed to be a *bean fasa* (wise-woman) who lived at Hill of the Grange, Co. Kildare.

The accounts cannot be all correct, but there is a similarity about the stories that cannot be denied.

For that matter, Dan Byrne, a 65-year-old resident of Aughrim, claimed to have some personal knowledge of the banshee who he said was a little woman with lovely hair. She cries like a child at twilight and at midnight, he said, though she was no harm to anyone. He added that she always combs her hair when crying.

Such are the little details that will lead a listener to nod in agreement with the storyteller, no matter how improbable the story might appear in daylight.

John Keogh, who currently lives a few miles further along the glen, relates a story of a girl of that place being sent out to mind a handful of cows belonging to the family. Fanciful or not, the girl reported that a troop of warriors clad in olden dress and carrying shields and spears passed her by, in single file.

'The last lad in the line told the girl that the brown cow in the corner needed milking and she should see to it as soon as possible', said John. 'And when she checked the animal the warrior was correct; but the troop was gone by the time she looked up.' Perhaps they were on their way to Avondale for a nap with the others.

A story of another girl being assisted by a stranger was told by Laurence Whelan from Knocanoocra, who was himself 77 years of age at the time of telling. A little girl was out walking one evening as the sun was setting. The evening was fair. Happy shadows were stretching across the roads before her and she was contented in herself, listening to the sounds of the countryside as she walked along.

Then coming towards her in the near distance she saw a group of little men with a big man stepping out in front of them as they walked along. She noticed they had a coffin in their hands, though it was not a large coffin. The girl stopped as they continued on towards her, for she had not encountered this before and was unsure as to what she was to do for the best.

The big man arrived at her feet first. He bent down with large hands and lifted her up onto the bank.

'Stay there until I come back for you', he said, not unkindly.

Well, whatever was on her she stayed there as they all passed her by and she was left with an empty road to stare at until the big man returned alone, a good two hours later, when there was not much light left in the place worth talking about. He lifted her back down again.

He said: 'The next time a funeral like that comes along, stay out of the way.' Then, he was gone, and when the girl looked around she was in her own paved farmyard, though she had been a distance away from home when she met the cortege.

Someone she confided in said it was a fairy funeral she'd seen passing and that it went to a different grave every night. Others say the Good People are immortal and do not have any use for a funeral, for they do not die.

It's the sort of occurrence that you will not believe until you see it for yourself.

And then it's a different story.

For seeing is believing and hearing is definitive, but telling is best.

If you enjoyed this book, you may also be interested in …

Dublin Folk Tales

BRENDAN NOLAN

Do you know who the real Molly Malone was or how the devil himself came to the Hellfire Club? These and many more accounts of Dubliners and Dublin City fill this book, as told by Brendan Nolan, a professional storyteller who has been recording these tales for decades. These are the stories of real Dublin, the stories that are passed from generation to generation and which give this city its unique character.

978 1 84588 728 5

Wexford Folk Tales

BRENDAN NOLAN

Wexford has a rich heritage of myths and legends which is uniquely captured in this collection of traditional tales. Discover the remarkable stories of the 140-year-old-man who died a premature death, the arrival of the antichrists (six of them) in Wexford, the dangers of love potions and how two people came back from the dead, together with tales of lurechan mischief, mermaids, grave robbing and buried treasure.

978 1 84588 766 7

Waterford Folk Tales

ANNE FARRELL

Anne Farrel takes the reader on a vivid journey through Waterford's folklore. Included are the tales of the legendary figures of Aoife and Strongbow, St Declan and the three river goddesses, together with stories of some of the less well-known characters such as Petticoat Loose, whose ghost is said to still roam the county, and the Republican Pig, who was unfortunate enough to become caught up in the siege of Waterford.

978 1 84588 757 5

Visit our websites and discover thousands of other History Press books.

www.thehistorypress.ie
www.thehistorypress.co.uk